A player no one expected to see . . .

Slowly, at the very back of the stage, a dark curtain began to open, creaking slightly. Slowly, the widening space between the curtains filled with a foglike mist. And from the fog appeared a player no one expected to see this year. A player no one expected to see ever again. Number Nine — Reggie Westerman.

Standing in the vaporous mist, circling and floating around it, the figure looked ten feet tall. A menacing hulk, shoulders padded to gigantic proportions, it loomed over the stage.

The entire assembly fell into a deadly silence.

Other Thrillers
you will enjoy:

Camp Fear
by Carol Ellis

The Cheerleader
by Caroline B. Cooney

The Train
by Diane Hoh

The Vampire's Promise
by Caroline B. Cooney

THE PHANTOM

BARBARA STEINER

SCHOLASTIC INC.
New York Toronto London Auckland Sydney

No part of this publication may be reproduced in whole or in part, or stored in a retrieval system, or transmitted in any form or by any means, electronic, mechanical, photocopying, recording, or otherwise, without written permission of the publisher. For information regarding permission, write to Scholastic Inc., 730 Broadway, New York, NY 10003.

ISBN 0-590-46425-6

12 11 10 9 8 7 6 5 4 3 2 1   3 4 5 6 7 8/9

Printed in the U.S.A.   01

First Scholastic printing, October 1993

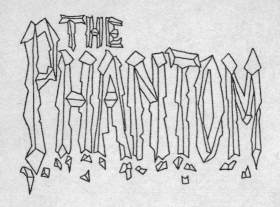

Chapter 1

"Are you all right, Jilly?" Amelia Seibert stood beside her best friend, ready to do what she could to help her.

But Jillian Hoff's ghostly white face, surrounded by white-blond hair, her haunted blue eyes, her stiff stance said she had taken a giant step backward. All the healing she had done over the summer had vanished.

"I can't do it, Mel. I can't go to the pep rally. Don't ask me to. Leave me alone." Jilly leaned forward against her locker in the cheerleaders' room off the gymnasium.

"I don't want to do that, Jilly. But I can't stay here. Come on. I'll be right beside you." Amelia took Jilly's arm and tugged gently.

Jilly shrugged it off. "No! I said no, I mean no. I'll just — I'll just go on home. Call me later. I promise I'll be all right."

Amelia stared at Jilly for a few seconds, an

1

ache swelling inside her chest. She pretended to be angry to get rid of it, then found the anger was real.

"Okay, fine. You do that. You go home. Go back into the self-pity you've enjoyed for almost a year. I can't help you anymore. I don't even want to try."

Turning, Amelia ran down the near-empty hall toward the auditorium. She bit her lip and sucked in air, trying to calm down. Her whole body started to shake. She could never get up in front of the entire school herself unless she got some control.

Ducking into a shadow in the back of the huge room, she leaned on the wall, surrounding herself with normal people and normal school activity.

Down front, the coach, some members of the team, and the rest of the cheerleading squad had gathered on the stage. A steady river of students streamed in, seniors filling the front rows. Sophomores hung back, still not sure of themselves, wondering if there was some protocol for seating in assemblies. Dozens milled about, visiting, others shouting at friends until teachers demanded a little order.

Amelia watched until she was fairly sure she could do this without going to pieces. Then, putting on a big cheery smile, she bounced down the aisle and climbed the steps to the stage.

"Amelia," Garth called, coming over to her when she turned, happy to hear his voice. "Where's Jilly?"

"I can't get her out of the locker room, Garth. She said at noon that she wasn't sure she could be here. She's not even sure she wants to stay on the cheerleading squad."

Garth took Amelia's arm, unconcerned about everyone watching them. "I don't blame her. I know how she feels. All summer I wondered if I could play football again. But when August training started, I knew I *had* to play. I had to play for Reggie. He wouldn't want me to stop."

"That's what I've tried to tell Jilly. She and Reggie loved each other. He wouldn't want her to grieve forever."

"You can't help her, Mel." Garth repeated what he'd said a million times. "I know you want to. You've tried. But you're giving up too much of yourself. Are *you* going to make it through the assembly?"

Amelia finally looked at him. His eyes said he cared. His hand on her arm said the same. She swallowed the lump in her throat and took a deep breath. "Sure. I'm ready. Let's get this show on the road." She glanced around to find the rest of the squad staring at them. Smiling, she gave them a thumbs-up signal. Everyone of them returned the gesture and smiled back. "Are *you* okay, Garth?" Amelia asked, focusing on this guy she was so crazy about.

"Yeah! If the word gets out that I broke training, I'm dead meat—benched for two games."

"We were studying, remember? Surely it's okay to study. You have to keep your grades up to stay on the team."

"I'm supposed to study at home, alone." Garth grinned. "What sacrifices I make for fame and glory."

"Not to mention fear." Amelia was only half-way teasing. Coach Joe Paladino was a legend in the tough, terrible teacher department.

"Look, Mel," Garth said suddenly. "What's Travis Westerman doing here?" Garth nodded his head to the front of the auditorium. Across the room, holding a pen and clipboard, was a tall, handsome man, totally the opposite coloring from his brother Reggie, but equally as good-looking. He had graduated from Stony Bay High a couple of years before.

"He's still writing the sports section of the *Daily*." Amelia stared at Reggie Westerman's brother as he spoke to a photographer, then left by the side door. "I guess that gives him a legitimate reason to be at the first pep rally."

"I can't believe he'd *want* to be here." Garth turned away, cuing Amelia to start the first cheer. As captain of the cheerleader squad, she ran the pep rallies. She realized that everyone was in place, waiting for her. She was grateful for their support.

"Gimme an S!" she shouted into the mike, getting the crowd's attention. Her squad, dressed in new black and gold sweaters, skirts or trousers, spread across the front of the stage. Sandy Sargent flashed a cue card with a huge black and gold S stenciled in the center.

"S!" shouted the assembled students, half-heartedly.

Amelia shook her head. "You can do better than that. Gimme another S!" She felt better. Yelling at Jilly hadn't helped. But yelling to arouse school spirit vibrated positive energy all through her body.

The crowd roared. The satisfying noise chased away the rest of her gloom. She went on to lead spelling out STONY BAY. Then she shouted the letters for BOMBERS, finishing the cheer. By the end of the final word, her team formed a pyramid, the top girls somersaulting off, while boys cartwheeled or split-jumped, demanding another deafening response. Amelia leaped up and punched the air, letting her hair bounce on her shoulders and swish around her face, sweeping away cobwebs from the past.

Next Amelia introduced Ms. Wiggens, their school principal. She was a popular math teacher, who had been promoted to head the school. She wore her hair in a bun, was pleasingly plump, and at first glance seemed meek and mild. With a booming voice, she changed her image. "Have we got a terrific football team? Are you going to have another winning year?" The crowd screamed. Ms. Wiggens started the next cheer.

Amelia finished it, then introduced Coach Paladino.

Coach said a few words about winning — no one was going to mention that four-letter word, *lose* — then motioned to Garth Dreyer, team captain, to take the mike.

"Vader, Vader, Vader," the crowd shouted Garth's nickname. He was never sure whether or not his parents had done him a favor giving him a name so close to the legendary villain. Not movie buffs, they said they hadn't realized what they were doing.

Amelia smiled at the look of panic on Garth's face. Playing football was fun, but Garth froze when speaking in front of a crowd. Amelia had helped him write a speech during their study session. But before he could open his mouth, he was interrupted.

Slowly, at the very back of the stage, a dark curtain began to open, creaking slightly. Slowly, the widening space between the curtains filled with a foglike mist. And from the fog appeared a player no one expected to see this year. A player no one expected to see ever again. Number Nine — Reggie Westerman.

Standing in the vaporous mist, circling and floating around it, the figure looked ten feet tall. A menacing hulk, shoulders padded to gigantic proportions, it loomed over the stage.

The entire assembly fell into a deadly silence.

Amelia stepped back, stunned, both hands covering her mouth to keep from screaming. A voice inside her kept yelling — kept shouting. But not cheers for a pep rally.

Over and over the voice screamed, *No, no, no! This is impossible. You're dead, Reggie, dead. I saw you die myself. I went to your funeral. I stood by your grave. For ten months you've lain in the Stony Bay Cemetery. You're dead, Reggie. Do you hear me? Dead!*

Chapter 2

Amelia watched, frozen, as if molded solid by a cold blast from the grave. Did she imagine a rank, foul odor, the stagnant smell of decay?

The figure swayed like a death puppet, held up only by invisible strings of dusty light beams. The golden helmet, like a polished human skull, moved slowly back and forth. The face mask, with its dark eye sockets, grinned through a bony, skeletal mouth. Surrounded by layers of velvet shadow, the player shimmered in the pale, gold moisture. Raising his arms, Reggie, black chest blazoned with a gold nine, claimed the stage, the audience, the moment of swelling awe. Then he pointed at Amelia and Garth, beckoning to them, *Come! Follow me back into my sweet, dense darkness.*

Amelia stretched both arms, palms out, warding off the temptation to walk toward him in an hypnotic slumber.

As a haze billowed around it, thicker and thicker, the player vanished into the smoke. Quickly, the back curtains slid closed, swishing along the floor. Rings at the top of the rod scraped like fingernails clawing at the inside of a coffin lid.

The first sound that reached Amelia's ears was a moan. She realized it was her own voice. Clasping her fist over her mouth, she bit off her cries. She listened instead to the shrieking audience. They had gathered to scream of victory but fear had joined the celebration.

Reggie Westerman was a player like Stony Bay had never seen before. With Reggie as quarterback, Stony Bay had won the regional and state championships two years in a row. With Reggie as team captain, school spirit had been the highest in Stony Bay history. Reggie's senior year was guaranteed to be his best. Not only would the Bombers win, but college scouts from all over the country would have attended every game.

But Reggie Westerman had gotten a spinal cord injury in the last game of the season. He lay in a coma, paralyzed, helpless. Two weeks later, Reggie had died. Now, for ten months, Number Nine had lain in a grave in Stony Bay's cemetery. For ten months, his friends, the whole school had mourned.

Today, he had returned.

"Reggie!" Coach Paladino shouted into the mike, trying to regain the crowd's attention. "Reggie! Reggie! Reggie!" He repeated the word, the ghost's name, over and over.

Finally, the crowd took up the chant. "Reggie! Reggie! Reggie!"

Memories gradually quieted the entire student body's panic. They pulled the Reggie they had known close enough to dispel the apparition that had taken shape before them. When they had rid themselves of the horror, replacing it with loving fervor for their fallen hero, Coach raised both arms, hands spread, gradually hushing the crowd.

Finally, there was absolute silence and he took advantage of the moment, letting the auditorium become as quiet as Reggie's grave.

"He could not stay away," Paladino began. "Our hero, who could not be here with us in reality, has chosen to remind us that he is with us in spirit. He will be with this fine team on the field for every game. We will not forget you, Reggie," the coach said, his voice taking on the timbre of an evangelist. He stretched his arm to its full length, reaching for the sky, as if his fingers were touching those of his fallen player. "I hereby dedicate this entire season to Reggie Westerman. Win for Westerman. Let's hear it, people. Win for Westerman!"

Caught in the emotion, the aftermath of a frightening specter, the students took up the chant. Three times they shouted the slogan. Three times the words echoed off the high ceilings and windowless walls of the auditorium.

"Win for Westerman!"

"Win for Westerman!"

"Win for Westerman!"

Continuing to be in charge, the coach signaled that the pep rally was at an end. Teachers filled the aisles, escorting a student body filled with passion outside to vent the rest of their feelings.

Comments floated on the highly-charged air.

"Wow, you think Coach planned that?"

"I think he staged it to get us revved."

Laughter. Whispers. Murmurs. Awe.

"Best pep rally I've ever seen."

"I think it was tacky. Really bad taste."

"I think Wiggens is going to kill him."

Laughter. Shouting. Shrieks. Anticipation.

As soon as Amelia could think, she felt empty and ashamed. How could Paladino do this? How could he make such a mockery of Reggie's death? How could he stage such a show and turn the pep rally into a tasteless, overly dramatic farce?

She felt anger rise from inside her like water nearing the boiling point, replacing her initial fear. But though she was half-afraid of Coach Paladino, she followed him as he herded his players off the stage.

Taking his arm, she bit off her words. "How could you do this, Coach Paladino? How could you take advantage of Reggie's death like that?"

He turned and stared at her. His face, pale as death itself, twisted with a frown. "I don't know what you're talking about, Amelia. But I tell you, no one is going to get away with that crass prank if I have anything to say about it. And you have no right to criticize my actions. I saved this day for us. In fact, someone may have done me a favor." His frown turned into a smile, and he hurried after his team.

Amelia was left alone. She turned and stared toward the back curtain, feeling goose bumps rise on her arms. A cold draft swirled about her legs, bare except for the tiny cheerleader's skirt and gold slouch socks.

A prank? She wanted to believe that was all

this scene had been. Someone with no taste whatsoever had planned this show. But she had no idea why it had been done. Still, there was one niggling thought that swirled around her mind, stirring up some atavistic fear from hundreds of years in her past. What if it wasn't a joke? What if — what if that really had been Reggie?

Her stomach knotted and spun as if she had just finished a series of cartwheels. Voices echoed all around her. "Reggie, Reggie, win for Reggie. Win for the ghost of Reggie."

What was wrong with her? She didn't believe in ghosts.

She staggered down the steep stairs into the auditorium and raced for the back, fleeing something she couldn't name. Running from something that couldn't possibly have happened.

Outside the big double doors, she bent over, drawing air into her aching lungs. She started for the girls' bathroom, when, out of the corner of her eye, she spotted Jilly.

Hesitating only a second, she spun around and hurried toward her. "Jilly, did you — where — "

Jilly leaned on the glass of a trophy showcase, looking as if she might be sick at any moment. She had been staring into it when Amelia first saw her. Now she bit her lip and accepted the hug from her best friend, hugging Amelia, too.

"I saw it, Mel. I was in the auditorium. I wanted to be on stage with you, but I couldn't, so I hung back, thinking maybe I'd join you later. It was awful, just awful. How could anyone do that? Who would do it?"

"I can't imagine, Jilly." Amelia continued to hold Jilly tight in her arms, patting her as if she were a baby. "I can't believe it happened."

Pushing Jilly away, Amelia dug in her waistband for the tissue tucked there. She blew her nose. "At first I thought Coach Paladino staged that."

"He got someone to pretend to be Reggie?" Jilly's eyes grew large and filled with tears. "Why, Mel, why?"

"So he could get the team fired up. You saw what he did."

"No, I ran out. I couldn't stay in there when — when — "

"He had people cheering for Reggie. He dedicated the season to him. Said they should win for Westerman."

"Oh, Mel, how could he?" Jilly's voice was angry now.

"He denied knowing anything about it, Jilly. He said he saved the day. That someone had pulled that prank, and he kept the situation from getting out of hand."

"He said it was a *prank*? What if it wasn't, Mel? What if Reggie did come back? What if he really was here with us today?"

"Jilly, come on. You can't *believe* that."

"Why can't I? I know it sounds strange to you, but it doesn't to me. I've felt Reggie with me all the time, ever since he — he — went on, he's been here in spirit. Sometimes I know he's right beside me. I feel him there. His love."

Amelia felt her stomach twist again, and tears welled up in her eyes. Poor Jilly. She stared at the glass trophy case and tried to get her own emotions in hand. It wasn't going to do any good for both of them to stand there and cry.

On display was Reggie's uniform. Here was his helmet, his shirt with the number nine, the number that was retired forever as far as Stony Bay teams were concerned.

The case had been dedicated to him after he

died. It had become a shrine for Jilly. If Amelia had been looking for her friend, she could have predicted that she'd find Jilly here, in front of this display.

There were a dozen pictures of Reggie. His junior photo, snapshots of him in action on the football field, newspaper headlines and articles about his skill, his achievements. Even the football from that last game. Signed by all the players, it balanced on end as if waiting for someone to kick off.

"Jilly, there you are. Are you all right?" A boy with dark, curly hair, only slightly taller than Jilly and Amelia, took Jilly's arm. Amelia couldn't help but notice the contrast in the two. Jilly was beautiful enough to be a New York model. Shelby Gunderson looked like a leftover from fifth grade.

"Sure, Gumby." Jilly searched her purse for a tissue. "I'll catch you later. I'm going home with Amelia."

Jilly seemed to gain some control all of a sudden, so Amelia was glad Shelby had walked up. But he was the last person Amelia had expected to see. Shelby Gunderson was senior class clown. Amelia held back a smile. The nickname Jilly called him — Gumby — fit him perfectly. He was a likeable enough guy, most of the time, a genius backstage at all Stony Bay's theater productions. But he wasn't one of Amelia's crowd. Nor, as far as she knew, was he a special friend of Jilly's. He hung out with the theater majors.

It was the tone of voice, rather than what Jilly said to Shelby that surprised Amelia. "You hanging out with Shelby now?" she asked, when Shelby disappeared out the backdoor, halfway hoping that Jilly would say yes. She'd been trying to get Jilly to start dating again. Shelby Gunderson wouldn't have been Amelia's choice for Jilly, but he was a start on recovering her social life.

"I will if I want to," Jilly said. "I like him. He makes me laugh."

Before Amelia could say she was glad someone could make Jilly laugh, another guy interrupted them. Travis Westerman was tall, lanky, with gray-blue eyes that changed quickly, depending on his mood. Now, they held a smile devoid of humor.

"Well, Jilly Bean, what did you think of that performance?" Travis slid a small notebook from his shirt pocket. "Have anything to say for the newspaper, to add to my story?"

Jilly stared at Travis. "What are you writing, Travis?"

"That just when we thought it was safe to stop worshiping my brother, he puts in another appearance. One quite dramatic, may I add. He would have enjoyed it, don't you think?" Travis's voice was sharp-edged.

"You'd like to forget that Reggie ever existed, wouldn't you, Travis?" Jilly said. "To forget that his star was so bright, you couldn't help but be a shadow. To forget that no one would ever remember *your* name if it hadn't been for Reggie. It doesn't matter what you tell your readers. They know the truth. Reggie will always be number one."

Travis's eyes turned icy steel. He spun around and marched toward the front door.

"Weren't you pretty hard on him, Jilly?" Amelia asked, watching Travis push through the double glass doors and run down the steps. "After all, he did lose a brother. I'm sure he loved Reggie as much as you did."

"I'm not sure. Reggie was just his ticket to all those great stories, the ones that got him that award for sportswriter of the year. I wouldn't put it past him to have staged the return of Reggie in order to get a story for his newspaper."

Amelia stared .at a disappearing Travis. "Jilly! You know he didn't do that. Listen, do go home with me tonight. Mom has to work late, and Dad is out of town. We'll order pizza. You'll go to the game, won't you? I don't think you should be alone."

Chapter 3

"Come on," said Amelia, walking toward the backdoor. "I have Dad's car." Looking up at the football uniform in the display case reminded her of the ghost, making her shiver.

Jilly hung back. Amelia watched as she kissed her fingers, touched the glass case at a spot nearest Reggie's junior photo, then turned and walked slowly toward Amelia.

"Jilly — "

"Don't ask me to forget him, Amelia. I can't. I just can't." Jilly's long blonde hair hung forward around her face like a mourning veil. But her blue eyes blazed with an eternal flame for a dead hero.

"I'm not asking you to forget Reggie, Jilly. I'd never do that. I'm — well, never mind. Let's go."

Amelia's ready temper flared. To tell the truth, she was tired of talking about Reggie

Westerman. She was tired of counseling Jilly, listening to her cry and threaten to commit suicide, say she didn't want to live without him. A tiny part of her wondered if by now, Jilly wasn't just being melodramatic.

Reggie hadn't been perfect. He and Jilly had fought and made up so many times everyone had lost count. But when someone dies you tend to remember only the good things.

They passed an open door leading to backstage in the auditorium. Voices drifted into the hall, angry voices.

Jilly frowned and stared at Amelia.

Amelia's curiosity overcame all her other emotions. "Let's see what's happening," she whispered, motioning to Jilly.

The draperies they pushed through gave off tiny particles of dust, smelling musty, ancient. Amelia shivered again. Did she feel something, or was it only a replay of the scene with Reggie?

Overhead, in the dim light, short curtains looked like families of bats clustered together, sleeping, their clawlike feet clinging to the brass rod. A remnant of fog remained as if caught between the scrim and the piled-up flats from last year's production of *Fiddler on the Roof*. The most visible flat was barren landscape with silhouetted trees, making the fog appear natural, though eerie.

Roberta Hodgekiss, the drama teacher, was the one who was practically shouting. Coach Paladino listened, his hands in his pockets as if keeping them trapped and in control. The principal, Ms. Wiggens, stood between them, placed in a position of referee.

"How could you do this, Pal?" Ms. Hodgekiss was saying. "It was a cheap trick, totally without taste, unforgivable."

"I tell you, Roberta, I *didn't* stage that scene. It was a complete surprise to me."

"I can almost believe you. You don't have that much imagination," Ms. Hodgekiss said. "But one of your players may have. We all know your job is on the line — that you probably won't have a winning year without Westerman. But come on, using Reggie Westerman like this is *sick*."

Amelia didn't see any way to sneak out, so she decided she'd better make her presence known. She stepped from the shadows into the faint overhead lighting. Jilly followed her.

"What are you two doing here?" Ms. Hodgekiss demanded.

Amelia was a little shaken by the tone of her voice. "We — I heard voices. I wanted to see how — " Then she stopped stuttering and spoke up. "If the coach didn't do this to boost school spirit, then who did?"

"Good question, Amelia," Ms. Hodgekiss replied. "That's what we're investigating ourselves. Jilly — I'm sorry about this."

"Thanks, Ms. Hodgekiss," Jilly said softly.

Amelia gave Ms. Hodgekiss credit for remembering that Jilly and Reggie had been going steady for two years. She would know that Jilly would be hurt by today's cheap shot.

Thinking she might be told to leave at any minute, Amelia did a quick examination of the stage area. "Look," she whispered to Jilly. "He stood on a box to look bigger. And the way the lights are slanted upward — that would make someone look taller."

Would a real ghost have to stand on a box? she asked herself. Or need spotlights?

On either side of where the ghost had appeared was a small plastic tub partially filled with water. A remnant of steam, or fog, hovered over the water.

"Dry ice." From behind Amelia, Ms. Hodgekiss answered her unvoiced question. "An easy stage trick for fog. And there are a dozen ways for someone to get out of here fast." She pointed. "That door leads to the parking lot. It should have been locked, but anyone could have opened it from inside during the day and left it open. That means anyone from the entire state of Michigan could have come in here, made an appearance, then left quickly. *If* you didn't do it, Pal."

Ms. Hodgekiss looked at Coach Paladino. Clearly, he was her top suspect. Backstage was her territory. She didn't like having it invaded. And it wasn't a secret that there was bad blood between the coach and the drama teacher. The school was small enough so that all the extra-curricular activities competed for bodies. Amelia had to choose between trying out for the first play and being on the cheerleading squad.

Cheerleading won, since there was nothing Amelia liked better than screaming her lungs out at football games. She loved football, loved Garth and all the guys, looked forward to every game. Until the final one last fall.

She knew this season was going to be different. But now someone had seen to it that it was not only different, but weird.

"Let's go." She nudged Jilly and fled the auditorium. "Let the teachers fight, or investigate, or worry — whatever they choose to do about today's drama. I want to forget it."

She shuddered as they left the school and

hurried across the school parking lot toward her dad's four-wheel drive Toyota.

"I don't know about you, Jilly, but I got the strangest feeling, remembering that scene. Course, you were way in the back of the auditorium, but I was right there in front of that — that — "

"Phantom of the team." Jilly finished Amelia's sentence. She giggled, then burst into tears. "Poor Reggie," she sobbed, half-laughing, half-crying. "Travis was right about one thing. He would have loved this."

Amelia smiled. "He would have, wouldn't he? If anyone pulled a practical joke, we all suspected Reggie. He probably got credit for a dozen tricks he *didn't* play on people."

They got quiet for a moment, remembering, while Amelia maneuvered out of her parking space and into the traffic on Eighteenth Street.

"Oh, Mel, it's going to be a terrible year. I don't know if I can stand it. Maybe I should have taken Mom up on going to Aunt Ruth's, living with her until college."

"No way, Jilly. We've dreamed of being seniors. We're going to have the most memorable senior year ever."

Maybe the Phantom *had* done them a favor. The opening of football season had freshened a lot of raw wounds. Reggie's appearance had gotten his death back out into the open and let them all cry about it one more time. Now they could move forward.

Win for Westerman! Why not?

"Let's go to Dexter's," suggested Jilly, just before they turned north to Amelia's home.

Dexter's Lakeside, right on the shore of Lake Michigan, was the hangout for the whole school. Since it was south of town, kids from other schools sometimes showed up there, too. Going there, being seen, would let Jilly say this hadn't defeated her. That if it was some kind of joke, she could take it.

"Great idea." Amelia swung the car left instead of right. "Let's find out how the rest of the world is reacting to Reggie's ghost."

Chapter 4

Music blared into the crowded parking lot. They weren't the only ones who'd decided to eat at Dexter's before the game. Amelia circled twice, then spotted a Chevy van pulling out. She waited, slid into the slot, and jumped out.

Both she and Jilly pulled on black and gold jackets. Dusk brought a cool breeze and a promise of moisture.

"I hope the rain will hold off until after the game," Amelia said, hurrying toward the front door.

The smell of fried fish, burgers, and the breadsticks that Dexter's was famous for, filled Amelia's nostrils. She was hungrier than she thought.

The minute that diners, mostly kids from school, spotted Jilly, they fell silent, as if holding their breath. Obviously she was the last person they'd expected to see come in.

Amelia squeezed Jilly's arm and whispered. "Not such a good idea after all?" Her comment really said, "Want to leave?"

"No way." Head held high, Jilly led Amelia to a booth set for two.

Amelia slid onto the cold plastic seat and grabbed the menu. Making a quick selection, she stared at Jilly. Her mascara was smeared around the corners of her eyes. Otherwise, she was as beautiful as ever.

Jilly glanced at Amelia, then played with her spoon. "Listen, Mel, Shelby wants me to drop the cheerleading squad."

"Drop cheerleading? But Jilly, it was the only thing we really wanted when we came into high school. I know it's hard, but . . . you aren't going to drop, are you? You can't." Amelia took Jilly's hand and squeezed it. "Listen, give it a chance. Think about it some more after tonight. I couldn't stand it if you dropped out, Jilly. You're my best friend, and we've always done everything together."

"Maybe it's time to *stop* doing everything together," Jilly said. "Everything is different this year. You know that. I don't want to be out there cheering for — for — the rest of them."

"It's still Reggie's team, Jilly. Nearly all the first-string are seniors. They've played together — with Reggie — for two years."

"And every one of them let Reggie down. If Garth had stopped Ralph Dougherty from tackling Reggie—if anyone would have stopped him — "

"You can't blame Garth, you can't blame anyone, Jilly. It just happened. Sometimes people get hurt playing football."

"People get hurt, but not killed." Jilly stared at the menu.

"It should never have happened, but it did. Reggie got tackled, he hit the ground wrong, he — "

"Let's talk about something else." Jilly turned to the waitress who interrupted them. "A spinach salad with poppy seed dressing."

"Is that all you're going to eat?"

"I'm not hungry."

"Who do you think dressed up like Reggie today, Jilly? And why?"

"If it wasn't Reggie — " Jilly paused as if still thinking it could have been. "Then it could have been anyone. The coach may have planned it to stir up the team. I wouldn't put it past Travis Westerman, though. Now that he doesn't have Reggie to create a great story for him, he'll create some himself."

"I heard he took Reggie's death pretty hard."

"He pretended to," Jilly replied. "He was always in Reggie's shadow. Now he realizes he needs Reggie. It was Reggie that made his life exciting. He's *nothing* without Reggie."

"Hey, ladies. Fueling up for the big game?" Had Shelby Gunderson followed them, or was it a coincidence that he was at Dexter's tonight, too?

"Gumby, sit down. Have you eaten?" Jilly smiled, moved over, although the booth was designed for two.

"I swallowed a burger. I thought you were going home with Amelia. If I'd have known you were coming here, I'd have waited. You want to go to Muskegon tonight, Jilly? There's a good horror film on."

"She has to be at the game, Shelby." Amelia answered for Jilly. "Aren't you going?"

"To watch a bunch of jocks pound each other

all evening?" Shelby grinned at Amelia, then looked back at Jilly. It was obvious he was crazy about her. "I have work to do for drama."

"Gumby thinks I can get the lead in the next play, Mel. That might be fun." Jilly took Shelby's hand and smiled at him.

"She could have gotten into this one if she'd have tried out." Shelby perched on the edge of the bench by Jilly and put his arm around her. When the food came, he stood up.

So did Jilly. "I'm too nervous to eat right now, Mel. Sorry. Give me a ride, Gumby. Then we can go someplace after the game."

Jilly tossed five dollars on the table and was gone before Amelia could think of any way to stop her. Shelby circled her waist with one arm, pushed the door open for her with the other. Jilly laughed way too much at something he said. Obviously, she was acting now in her own play.

Amelia looked at her fries. They glistened with grease. Her burger was pink in the center, just the way she liked it, but the cheese was already congealing around it. She mashed the top down, picked it up, took one bite. The ground beef tasted dry, like sawdust. It took her a long time to chew it well enough to swallow.

Sipping the Pepsi, she decided she couldn't eat, either. Taking her drink, she left the rest of the food on her plate.

No doubt about it — it was going to be a very long football season.

Chapter 5

School spirit that night was the highest Amelia could remember. And there was the biggest crowd. By now, everyone in town had heard about the pep rally ghost. Had people come to see if Reggie would make another appearance at the game?

The threat of rain vanished. The night turned into perfect Indian summer weather. The field blazed with light. The air crackled with electricity, not generated by the huge posts with their multispots. Neither Amelia nor the rest of the cheerleaders had to work hard to get people to yell.

Amelia found she was on edge. Was she, too, waiting, watching? But Jilly seemed more at ease, arriving at the last moment, laughing with Shelby. She didn't act like the old Jilly, but she did seem to be having a good time.

Jilly was the one who reminded the student

section of their new slogan. "Win for Westerman!" She lifted her megaphone and shouted at the end of the first cheer.

"Win for Westerman!" the crowd yelled. They started the first wave. As if they'd been coached, each part of the wave echoed "Win!" as they stood and threw both hands upward, leaning toward the next section of bleachers. The second time around, the wave echoed "Westerman."

"This is incredible," Amelia said to Jilly as she grabbed a water bottle to wet her dry lips and throat. "If we don't win tonight, it won't be because the fans aren't behind the team."

"It's almost as if Reggie's here with us, isn't it?" Jilly spoke with a sense of awe.

Amelia grabbed Jilly's hand. "He is, Jilly. He is."

The Bombers would win, without a doubt. But at halftime the score was tied. Bernard Downing, star linesman for the Mountaineers, was everywhere, an efficient tackling machine. He was not intimidated at all by rumors that tonight, the Bombers had supernatural help, a twelfth player on the field.

He tackled Buddy Nichols twice for a big loss of yardage. He decked Garth, carrying the ball, a couple of times. Maybe that just spurred the Bombers on. They ran away with the second half, whipping Storm Mountain thirty-eight to seventeen.

Buddy Nichols had replaced Reggie as quarterback. To everyone's surprise he was almost as good as Reggie. He'd been backup for so long, a shadow to Reggie, that he'd never had a chance to prove himself. The crowd realized that now. In the last quarter, the words in the wave changed. "Win," the crowd yelled first. But the second time around, they shouted, "Nichols."

Garth had been moved to wide receiver, a position which suited his size much better than being on the defensive line. He was all over the field. He caught two touchdown passes and ran them in by himself. He was sure to be voted most valuable player, unless it was a tie with Buddy.

The cheerleaders lined up to create a human tunnel for the tired team to run through as the final buzzer sounded.

Amelia held out her hand for Garth to slap as he jogged by. "See you later," she called, and he nodded.

"You going with us tonight to Dexter's?" Amelia asked Jilly when the team had disappeared into the dim passageway that led to the locker rooms.

"No, and please don't ask me to do that, Mel." Jilly shook her head.

Amelia stared at Jilly, trying to decide how much to push her. "Okay, but if I announce a beach party for tomorrow night to celebrate our winning, will you help me plan it?"

Jilly appeared to think it over. "I guess so. If Shelby will help us, too."

"Is he going to start hanging out with us jocks instead of the theater majors?" Amelia teased.

"Ask him yourself." Jilly giggled. "He's standing right behind you."

Amelia felt her face get hot as she turned and looked into Shelby's eyes.

He took Jilly's arm, suggesting that they might have been going together longer than Amelia realized.

Jilly smiled at Shelby and whispered something to him. Was that the same smile that had once been reserved for Reggie? Not quite, Amelia decided, if she were any judge of Jilly's smiles. And she was, since they'd been friends forever.

Jilly's mother and Amelia's mother ran a gift

and antique shop for the tourists who jammed the lake towns in summer. Jilly's father commuted to Chicago to run one of the television stations there.

"I hope the crowd wasn't disappointed that our ghost didn't reappear tonight," Amelia joked.

"You think that's why they came?" asked Jilly.

"Not the only reason." Shelby pushed her playfully. "Some people will actually pay to watch a bunch of jocks try to kill each other."

Amelia defended the Bombers. "In case you haven't noticed it, Shelby, football is a popular sport. And the Bombers are a terrific team. They've never played so well. They've pulled the team back together beautifully this fall. And, I think whoever staged that little event in assembly this afternoon did us a favor."

"Rumor has it it was Coach Pal's idea," Shelby said.

"Did he have to be so dramatic about it?" Amelia asked. "Why not just say, 'Hey, guys, remember Reggie? We should dedicate this season to him.'" Amelia shivered, remembering how scared she'd been.

"You'll have to admit he got everyone's attention with the performance." Shelby laughed. "But he didn't need to do it again. He had his team conned. Having the ghost show up tonight might've distracted them. I think it was a great trick."

"It was such a shock having Reggie up there." Jilly's voice trailed off.

Amelia changed the subject quickly. "Want to help us plan a beach party for tomorrow night, Shelby? We need to celebrate tonight's win." She didn't particularly like Shelby, but if Jilly did, she'd try.

"Rehearsals for the senior play don't start till Monday. I guess I could. Ready, Jilly?" Shelby took her hand and tugged her toward the parking lot.

Amelia felt lonely watching Jilly leave with Shelby. She and Garth, Jilly and Reggie, had always gone out after the games to celebrate, win or lose. And with Reggie as quarterback, the team never even thought of losing.

She could go into the cheerleaders' locker room and change, but she huddled outside, just at the edge of the stadium. She didn't want to go into the school alone.

She pulled her coat tighter and watched as one by one the big lights darkened. Shadows took over the field. Echoes of the crowd's screaming bounced around in her head. Suddenly it was much too quiet. Standing, she paced back and forth along the fence.

"Miss me?" A voice made her jump.

"Oh, Garth. What took you so long?" She fell into his arms.

"You *did* miss me, didn't you? I could have taken longer. Reporters, backslapping, reliving the game. You know — all that hoo-rah-rah."

"I know I was out here alone." She hated being grouchy, but she had spooked herself waiting.

"Sorry, Mel." He bounced a kiss off her forehead. "I didn't know that or I'd have sneaked off. Not a bad game, was it?"

An allover warmth pushed away the remains of Amelia's willies at being alone in the stadium. "Not bad at all. Ready to celebrate?"

Before Garth could answer, Travis Westerman appeared out of nowhere, as if he'd been watching them, waiting for Garth.

"Well, you guys got lucky tonight, Dreyer. Have anything to say to the press?" Travis switched on a tiny recorder, about the size of a cigarette pack, and pushed it under Garth's nose.

Garth slammed it aside. "Luck had nothing to do with our winning, Travis. You know enough about football to have seen that."

"How come Pal didn't put you in as quarterback? Have any resentment about his decision?"

"Of course not. Buddy Nichols did a great job. He was perfect for the position. Paladino knows what he's doing."

"It would seem so. But I hope he won't forget who made his reputation for the last couple of years. He'd be at Podunk High by now if it hadn't been for Reggie." Travis spun around and headed for a black T-bird, one he'd restored to mint condition.

"Is that true, Garth?" Amelia asked. "That Reggie *was* the team. That he made Paladino look good?"

"We've had to make some adjustments, Mel. There's a lot of difference in hanging out, letting one guy do all the work and get all the glory — and in everyone's working together. I've realized something this year, though. I'm not even sure I *liked* Reggie Westerman."

Amelia thought about what Garth said. It didn't surprise her. Reggie was always stuck on himself, but he was so carefree and devil-may-care, everyone liked him anyway. Or pretended they liked him.

"We've already started planning a beach

party tomorrow night to celebrate," Amelia said, changing the subject.

"Great. You know, Mel, when Reggie appeared on the stage with us this afternoon, I felt sick. I'm never going to get over thinking that if I'd have stopped my man that night, Reggie would never have gotten hurt."

"Garth — "

"I know, I've told myself a million times it wasn't my fault. But in a way, it was. Ralph Dougherty was my responsibility to tackle."

"He must weigh three hundred pounds, Garth." Amelia argued the way she had several times before when Garth had relived the night Reggie got hurt. "You didn't even belong in that position. You've proved it tonight."

"Pal says he thinks that stunt in assembly today was pulled off by some of the Lakers' team. To destroy our confidence. If we started out the season losing, by the time we got to them, we'd be fish bait."

Amelia laughed at the idea. "Did he say who?"

"No, but we've heard that Ralph Dougherty will do anything on a dare. His teammates are always putting him up to some dumb trick."

"That would never have occurred to me. But Ms. Hodgekiss said the backdoor to the stage was unlocked, and that anyone from the whole state of Michigan could have gotten in. If that was what happened, their plan backfired, didn't it?"

"It sure did. We're rolling. The only way the Lakers can take the district now is if they beat the Mountaineers, *and* us, *and* win all the rest of their games. Tonight is going to come back to haunt them for the rest of the season."

While Reggie haunts us, Amelia thought.

Chapter 6

Amelia talked to people at Dexter's about the beach party, then made some phone calls the next morning. For a moment, her hand wavered, thinking about Jilly. Will Jilly have changed her mind? What mood will she be in today? She was tired of being so careful of Jilly's feelings.

Grabbing the phone, she punched in Jilly's number. If Jilly had made other plans, fine. Amelia resolved not to care.

"That sounds like fun, Mel." Jilly answered her invitation without hesitation. "And Shelby wants to come. We talked about it last night."

Amelia relaxed. "You really like him, don't you, Jilly?"

"Yes. Maybe because he's so different. He's not at all like Reggie. I don't have to keep being reminded of what was or might have been. I think he likes me."

"I'm sure he likes you, Jilly. Who doesn't? Want to bring chips or some hot dogs?"

"I'll make a cake. That okay?"

"Sure. Want us to stop for you? Garth and I are going early to claim a spot. Bring some wood, too, so we can have a bonfire."

"Okay, but don't pick me up. Shelby has a car, if you want to call it that." Jilly seemed in a splendid mood.

Amelia forgot her annoyance and felt like shouting, "Hooray, the old Jilly is back." She decided to stop balancing on a tightrope every time she talked to Jilly, to stop treating her as if she might break into a million pieces at any minute. That might be what Jilly needed — everyone to act normal — in order for *her* to return to normal. People tend to be what you want them to be or what you expect them to be. Amelia realized that what she really wanted was for Jilly to be like she was before Reggie died. That was impossible, so she'd stop expecting it.

"Okay, any time after four. A bunch of people said they're coming early to swim." Amelia hung up and started to plan her own evening.

The phone rang while she stood staring into her closet. Expecting someone with a question about the party, she answered.

"I have the rest of the day off, Dad's boat, and my car running," said Garth. "What else could a beautiful woman ask for?"

Amelia laughed. "Half an hour to pack a lunch and get my suit on."

Garth worked at his father's boat dock almost every weekend. His whole family put in seven days a week all summer, making enough money off tourists to get them through the long winters. Then Garth's dad worked on engines and a boat he was building. Mrs. Dreyer made crafts to sell in her gift-snack-boat shop the next season. The lake communities were almost equally divided between people who ran the resorts and stores and people like the Hoffs who lived in the big homes with lake views and commuted to high-paying jobs in Chicago. There were almost as many private planes in the area as there were cars.

"Use most of that time for the lunch, please. I'm starved, and I've got to get out of here before Dad changes his mind."

"He liked the game?" Amelia asked.

Garth's dad was his biggest fan, but he was also a perfectionist. He pushed Garth to be perfect in everything he did. When the Bombers won, he softened up enough to be easy on Garth for a couple of days. Garth knew how to take advantage of the situation.

"I can't do any wrong. For a couple of days, at least."

Amelia hung up and scrambled, throwing clothes, sunscreen, hat, lunch — all into a big faded, woven tote her aunt had sent her from Mexico. She loaded her food for the party into a picnic hamper and soft drinks into a cooler. Making three trips, she reached the curb at the same time that Garth clattered up. His old Chevy didn't hum like a 'Vette or a well-oiled boat motor, but it was transportation.

Garth gave Amelia a quick kiss, then helped her load the cooler and basket. He slid into the driver's seat, shifted into reverse, and squealed away from the curb.

The old car groaned and wheezed, as Garth swung onto Interstate 31 and up to Little Sable Point where his family kept their rental boats.

"Tonight will be as light as day. There's a full moon," Garth said as they ferried supplies from the car to the small sloop named, playfully by Garth's family, *The Garth Vader*. "If there's any wind at all, we'll sail back."

Amelia sighed. "I just want to have fun. I want to forget Friday's assembly ever happened, Garth. Never in my life have I been so scared."

"I've already decided it was a really dumb prank. Whoever planned it didn't think about the pain they were causing Jilly or the consequences for any of us who knew Reggie."

A little voice inside Amelia said, *Or did they?* But who would deliberately hurt Jilly and stir up bad feelings at Stony Bay High School? Well, so much for resolutions. It took all the control she had to force her mind away from the subject. *Get to work.*

Quickly they untied the mainsail and pulled it aloft. Facing into the wind, Garth tacked until the sail billowed outward. The breeze in her face, Amelia gloried in the fresh air for a short time.

"I see Reggie's boat is still in your dock, Garth. Do any of the Westermans use it?" she asked. Reggie had loved sailing only second to football. He'd worked to buy his own boat. The last two summers, he and Jilly had practically lived on it.

"Travis occasionally. But he keeps talking about selling it. Says he doesn't like to sail. In fact, he confided in me once that he's a poor swimmer. Afraid of the water. Can you imagine?"

"I can't. I don't remember *learning* to swim. I figure I was born knowing how." Amelia leaned out, balancing the sloop. She watched the sun sparkle off the waves, dragged her hand in the lake.

Finally being on the water did its job. The wind swept her hair out like a tiny sail, clearing her mind of any cobwebs left from the past day's events.

Two state parks slid by, then the pioneer village where Amelia had worked the past two summers, pretending to go back in time for tourists who wanted a glimpse of history.

Ludington State Park spread out along the shoreline. The seniors had a favorite spot where they liked to party. Garth maneuvered sails to slow the sloop as Amelia steered close.

They moored the boat just off a sandy beach, unloaded the cooler and picnic basket onto a couple of tables to reserve them. Garth piled his cooler and a couple of grocery sacks near a grill and fire pit to lay claim to it.

Almost immediately, a voice carried over the lake. "Hey, deadheads, race you."

"It's Jilly!" Amelia ran to the water. She was surprised by how pleased she was to see Jilly. "With Shelby. Can you believe that?"

"Yes, I can." Garth pretended to be really

disappointed. "Just when I had you all to myself."

Amelia laughed and ran to help Jilly pull their sloop in beside *The Garth Vader*.

"Hope we aren't interrupting anything," Shelby shouted. He jumped into the shallow water, then reached back for a cooler twice the size of Amelia's.

Amelia realized she hadn't seen Shelby without his shirt in a long time. He'd been counselor in some drama camp most of the summer. Her remark slipped out before she realized it might be a put-down.

"What have you been doing, Shelby, lifting weights?"

As small as he was, Shelby was no longer a wimp. He had muscles piled on top of muscles in his chest, his arms, and legs.

"I'll ignore the *way* you said that, since rah-rah girls are known snobs." Shelby did a couple of Mr. Universe poses.

"You should have come out for football. We could have used a little more muscle on the line this year." Garth reached for a second box of groceries.

"I'm not that dumb." Shelby balanced a sack on his head and waded to the nearest table.

"How did you have time to bake a cake, Jilly,

then buy all these groceries, *and* sail out here so fast?" Amelia asked, watching Jilly pose on the front of her father's sloop, looking like an old-fashioned figurehead.

"Oh, I didn't. Gumby convinced me it was much too nice a day to stay in the kitchen."

"And Daddy's boat beckoned." There was a put-down-the-rich tone in Shelby's voice. Amelia knew he lived with his mother, who waited tables at one of the nicer restaurants on the bay.

She wondered again what Shelby was doing here. Maybe "Daddy's" money beckoned to him to help make life easier.

Meow, Amelia said to herself. "Last one out of the bay is a beached whale." She ran for *The Garth Vader*.

Jillian's Dream trailed until they caught the wind. Then Jilly threw out a yellow and orange spinnaker, and they pulled ahead quickly.

"No fair," Garth shouted as Jilly whizzed past.

"Tough," Jilly screamed back.

The glorious afternoon raced away, catching the wind to best advantage. The two couples slid back into the sandy port reluctantly, anchoring in the shallows, wading to shore.

Car doors slammed as other seniors arrived.

Voices chased away marauding gulls. Squeals of laughter floated across the sunset. Buddy Nichols and Frank Evans started building a huge bonfire.

"Why is Jilly Bean with the Gunderson dweeb?" asked Frank. "If she's ready to join the world again, she can do better than that."

"Maybe you aren't her type, Frankie-pankie." Buddy said.

"Leave her alone, guys." Amelia stopped the comments. "At least she's out here instead of at home moping."

As evening darkened and a moon like a hon-eyed saucer slid up the sky, wood smoke filled the air. The smell of hot dogs roasting and ham-burgers sizzling made Amelia aware that she was starving.

"Let's swim again before we eat," Garth suggested, pulling her to her feet. "It's still as warm as mid-August."

Amelia had cutoffs over her suit, but it was still damp. She kicked off the shorts, and let Garth tug her into the shallows.

Playfully they splashed and kicked water at each other before going deeper and diving. Buddy Nichols caught up with Garth and ducked him, trying to hold him under the water.

"Watch out for the Creature from the Black Lagoon," teased Buddy's steady, Sandy Sargent. She waved at them, but stayed out of Buddy's reach.

Amelia started to wave back, make a smart remark, when she realized that Sandy had frozen, her face reflecting disbelief. Raising her arm slowly, Sandy pointed.

Screams ripped the soft night air.

Grabbing Garth's arm, Amelia whirled around. Her body turned to ice. *No, oh, no, please, not again!*

About thirty feet away, down the beach from them and silhouetted against the moon, Reggie Westerman slowly rose from the lake.

Chapter 7

For a few seconds, Amelia could only stare. The football player seemed to be ten feet tall. Backlighted by the moon, Reggie glowed with an unholy aura. Slimy weeds draped over his helmet, dripping diamonds of lake water. Eye sockets in his mask were dark holes, but she could feel him staring at her.

Firelight flickered off the front of the uniform, causing all the gold trim and the number nine to shine as if phosphorescent.

For those same seconds the night held its breath, surrounding them with a tomblike silence. Then a wave rushed in, its silky claws raking the sand as it rolled back, whispering when no one else dared speak.

Amelia felt a scream start deep inside her, rise to squeeze her lungs, scald her throat. Her voice filled the quiet.

Still screaming, she stumbled back into

Garth's arms, grabbing Buddy's hand. The figure raised one gloved hand and pointed straight at them. No words came from the skeletal mouthpiece, but the unspoken threat filled her with dread, stuffing her mouth and throat and chest with dark, smoky cotton. She choked, felt her stomach ache and churn.

The player seemed to be either singling the three of them out or accusing them — it wasn't clear which.

Then, melting into the silver runway the moon provided, the specter slowly disappeared beneath the water. Concentric circles started where the helmet disappeared, traveling farther and farther out until they splashed and sucked at Amelia's bare feet.

When the lake closed over the top of the helmet, everyone felt free to speak. There were shouts, screams, confused babbling, but at first no one made any attempt to follow the creature back into its watery grave. Then Buddy and Frank dived, along with another shadow swimmer from beside Jilly's boat.

As soon as the word entered Amelia's mind, it echoed over and over. Grave, grave, grave — Reggie belongs in his grave.

She spun around and pressed her face against Garth's chest to rid herself of the sight and the sounds inside her head. She held him tightly to keep him from swimming off after Reggie. Sobbing softly, she clutched him until she gained control.

"What was it, Garth? What was it?!" she gasped, pulling back and staring at his pale face.

"Don't you mean who? Who was it?" There was anger in Garth's voice. "This wasn't funny the first time it happened. Now it's even less so."

"Who do you think it was, Dreyer?" asked Buddy, returning, dripping with fishy-smelling weeds. "The water's as murky as a sewer. He disappeared before we could spot him again."

Frank shook himself like a dog, his long hair swinging water toward them. The third swimmer, to Amelia's surprise, was Shelby. He surfaced, stood, stared at them. He said nothing, but hurried off into the shadows.

"Who would do this, Garth?" Amelia asked. "And why?"

Garth shook his head slowly. "I have no idea, but why didn't I go after him? He wasn't that far away. Why did I stand here and watch?"

"Oh, Garth, we all stood here and watched that — that thing come and go. You can think now that you should have gone after it, but Buddy and Frank didn't find anything."

"What if — what if it's not someone," stuttered Sandy Sargent. "I mean, what if it's real?"

"A real ghost?" Debby Rollins shook her head. "I don't believe in ghosts."

"I didn't either . . . before this," Amelia whispered.

"There's nothing supernatural about that appearance. Someone is inside that uniform." Garth's anger was growing. He seemed ready to dive in, to swim after the football player.

"Come on, G-Garth." Amelia stuttered and her teeth clicked together. "Let's get out of the water. I'm freezing." She held tight to Garth, afraid he would still go after Reggie. Then she started to shiver, getting Garth's attention quickly. Taking her hand, he pulled her to the bonfire.

"Stay right here. I'll get you a sweater." He turned and hurried to where she'd left her tote.

"Who do you think it was, Amelia?" Sandy asked, her voice still shaky. "Do you think it's real? Why do you think he pointed to you and Garth and Buddy?"

"This is intense." Frank Evans wrapped his

hair in a towel and voiced his excitement. "I might have known old Reggie would come back to haunt us."

Everyone tried to laugh at Frank's remark, but the sound faded into the wood smoke quickly, rising on the heat to be forgotten.

Amelia grabbed the sweater that Garth handed her and tugged it on. As she warmed up, her brain started to function again. "Where's Jilly? Is she all right?" Then she looked from group to group, faces of friends all melting together. Farther and farther out she searched until her eyes rested on the picnic table farthest from the fire. Someone had wrapped an old blanket around Jilly. She huddled at the table, cold and wet and obviously miserable. Her face was buried in her hands, elbows propped on her knees.

An opening cleared as Amelia ran to her, sat beside Jilly, and circled her shoulders with her arm, pulling her close.

"Jilly, are you all right?"

"Why, Mel, why is Reggie doing this?"

"It's not Reggie. Don't even *think* that way. It's a joke, Jilly, a sick joke from some deranged mind." Amelia looked around. "Who has a car to take Jilly home? And who sails? Someone needs to take her sloop back to Little Sable."

"I'm okay, Mel, really I am." Jilly raised her head, wiping her face with the back of one hand. "Daddy doesn't like just anyone sailing his boat. Shelby and I will get it back."

At the mention of his name, Shelby, wrapped in a beach towel, stepped from the shadows. He acted as if nothing out of the ordinary had happened.

"Did you see anything out there, Shelby?" Amelia asked. "In the water, or just now?"

"Sure. Some gonzo tried to freak us out. And me without my video camera. Pretty good special effects, but it didn't work, except to upset Jilly. You want to go home, Jilly Bean?" He called her the nickname lots of people used to tease her.

"No, I'm fine. Let's get something to eat." Jilly rose, tossed off the blanket, and headed for the bonfire.

"Maybe Reggie's jealous. This is pretty strange. I never had a ghost jealous of me before." Shelby, his face pale, followed Jilly.

"Good for you, Jilly." Buddy Nichols stepped in beside her. "I had a wiener roasted almost to perfection. It's yours if we can find it."

With Jilly's declaration, everyone returned to preparing food or eating what they'd started. It appeared that the party was going to go on as planned.

Not as planned, Amelia thought, but if everyone else could pretend that nothing had happened, she'd try. Her eyes kept returning to the lake, though, with its whispers about what it was hiding.

Reggie, the waves whispered. *Reggie is down here, waiting. Come and swim. Dive deep. The water makes a comfortable grave. I'm waiting. I'm waiting for you, Amelia. You and Garth and Jilly. We can be a foursome again. Come . . . come. . . .*

"No!" screamed Amelia. "No!"

"Mel?" Jilly took her arm. "It's okay. He's gone. He went back. I guess he wished he was at the party. He was always the life of the party."

"Stop it, Jilly!" Amelia squeezed her arm. "Just stop that. Stop talking about Reggie as if he could come back."

"Well, he did, didn't he?" Frank tried to laugh, then choked on the liquid in his paper cup. It smelled suspiciously of alcohol.

"Want a brew, Mel?" said Frank. "Jilly?"

"No, Frank. It won't help, nothing will

help." Amelia shoved his hand away.

"I don't drink, Frank," answered Jilly. "You know that."

"Coach will know, Frank," teased Buddy. "He knows all, sees all, hears all."

"Only if someone rats on me." Frank laughed again, spewing liquid onto the fire, making it hiss.

Garth threw wood on the blaze, not worrying about how big it got or how hot. It was as if the bigger the fire they built, the safer they'd be.

Flames will keep away wild beasts, won't they? Will fire keep away ghosts? Those who return from the dead, determined to haunt the ones they left behind.

After a few minutes, where a soft, whispered sense of awe filled the air, the crowd made a pretense of forgetting — ignoring Reggie. They jostled and laughed, pushed and shoved and punched.

"Ghost boogie," Jerry Michael shouted. "Guaranteed to exorcise spooks." He switched on his battery-driven boom box and ran the volume up to earsplitting. The night blared with a Blues Traveler tape. A harmonica moaned and the drumbeats vibrated all through Amelia's body.

She felt cold, so cold, and moved to stand closer to the fire, to Garth and Buddy, who were cooking hot dogs. "How can they just forget what happened?"

"They haven't forgotten, Mel," Buddy assured her. "They're ignoring it. No one wants to admit to being afraid."

Someone bumped Amelia, and she stumbled toward the fire. "Hey, watch it," she snapped.

"Sorry," someone shouted. "Sorry, sorry, sorry." It turned into a chant.

The music became frenzied. Everyone screamed, shouted, wiggled, shoved, bounced. Bodies got closer, closer, closer, pressing Amelia closer and closer to the bonfire, smothering her with a wave of rising hysteria.

"I'm moving, guys." She turned to Buddy and Garth.

One minute Buddy was roasting a wiener, the next he was tumbling, flying toward the fire.

"Buddy!" Amelia screamed, feeling as if something held her rooted to the sand, kept her from grabbing him.

"Watch out!" Garth tried to catch Buddy, to push him away from the flames. But Buddy stumbled and fell, his dry shirt flaring around him, turning him into a human torch.

"Buddy! Get him out of there!" screamed Sandy. "He's on fire!"

Hands from all around grabbed, pulled, rolled Buddy onto the sand, away from the bonfire. Someone threw a beach towel. Garth snatched it from the air and wrapped it around Buddy to smother the flames. Another damp towel finished the job.

Buddy moaned and gave out little screeches of pain. "Help me, help me, someone help me," he whispered in a small voice like a child, calling to his mother from a nightmare. He writhed and twisted. The odor of burnt hair and flesh floated around him.

"Buddy, Buddy, Buddy, oh my baby." Sandy knelt beside him, not knowing whether or not to touch him.

Crouching beside Sandy, Amelia clutched her shoulders. "He'll be all right, Sandy. He'll be all right."

She lied. She knew she lied. How could flesh seared and puckered, blacked into charcoal edges ever be all right?

"Who has a car?" shouted Garth, taking charge. "We'll get him to the hospital."

This is a nightmare, thought Amelia. *I'll wake up in just a few seconds.*

"Put him in the back of my van," said Kristin Lloyd.

"Take him to the hospital in Muskegon," someone suggested. "They have a burn center."

"I'm going, too. I'm not leaving Buddy." Sandy, face wet and stained with soot and tears, followed the towel-wrapped body, crawled in beside him.

Amelia watched the crowded van back out and pull away. "Is he going to die, Garth? Is Buddy going to die?" All her strength had drained away, leaving her lifeless. She collapsed on the sand, rubbing her hands in the gritty soil until they stung.

"I don't know, Mel, I don't know," Garth whispered. But his next words, spoken almost in a whisper, frightened her worse than death.

"I was standing beside Buddy. His face . . . his look of surprise. He didn't stumble into that fire, Mel. He acted as if someone . . . *pushed* him. I tried to catch him. I reached for him. I tried. I couldn't . . . I just couldn't."

"Oh, Garth, no. Don't say that. I was standing there, too. I didn't see anyone near Buddy. Someone bumped me. I nearly fell. That's why I was going to move."

"Maybe I'm wrong." Garth leaned his head into both hands.

"You are, Garth. I'm sure you are." Amelia stood and moved to take Garth's arm. "No one pushed Buddy."

"No, Mel, wrong about the ghost. There's no one — nothing alive — inside Reggie's uniform. You saw how fast that thing disappeared into the water. Without a trace. That thing is — *is* a ghost." Garth shook his head back and forth as if he couldn't believe what he was saying. "It came back. It pushed Buddy."

Amelia said slowly, "Maybe it *was* Reggie. Maybe he's jealous of how well Buddy filled his position as quarterback. It's Reggie, Garth. It's really Reggie. Maybe he's saying that no one can take his place, Garth, no one!"

Chapter 8

Frank staggered out of the bushes in time to hear what Garth and Amelia had said. He was pale, but he was cold sober.

"God, this is awful. And I feel awful." He held his head, still looking sick. "But what are you talking about, Vader? Everyone was horsing around. Nobody pushed Buddy on purpose. Especially no ghost."

Garth took a deep breath and shook his head, as if trying to return to reality. "Yeah, you're right, Frank. This is crazy. Let's go home, Mel." He hurried to gather up their gear, leaving Amelia and Frank staring at him.

"Whew! *Garth* is crazy," said Frank, staring at the fire. No longer popping cheerfully, it had turned to coals and ash. Wisps of smoke still gave off an acrid smell. "What do you think, Mel?"

Why did people keep asking her — she

wasn't any expert on ghosts. "I don't know what to believe. I didn't *see* anything."

"That tells you something right there," Frank concluded.

"It does not!" Amelia's temper flared. "Do you really believe that Reggie's ghost is following us around? That he came to this party and pushed Buddy into the fire?"

Amelia had just gotten through saying that maybe he did, that maybe there was a ghost. But the rational part of her refused to keep believing it.

"Hey, don't yell at me. It's not my fault."

"Of course not. You just want to get drunk and forget it."

Frank crumpled up on the sand and cradled his head in his hands. "I'm paying — I'm paying."

Amelia folded up beside him, letting Garth load their things. "I'm sorry, Frank. I'm worried about Garth. Now he thinks he should have kept Buddy from falling into the fire and he still feels guilty about Reggie."

"No one else thinks Garth could have protected Reggie. That's all in his head. But one thing's for certain. If someone really did push Buddy, it wasn't any ghost."

"Why would anyone want to hurt Buddy?"

Amelia felt sick again remembering Buddy begging for help.

Frank shrugged. "Jealousy? Or to hurt the team? Something we don't know about?"

"There's too much going on that we don't know about. We're going home, Frank. Can you drive?"

"No. I'll get someone to drive my car."

People stood in little clumps whispering or crying. Some packed up, while others loaded cars.

Amelia stood and waded out to Garth's sloop.

The romantic, moonlight sail back to Stony Bay turned into a long, subdued trip. Several times, Amelia caught sight of Jilly and Shelby keeping pace with them, but there were no shouted challenges, no laughter or hollering back and forth, playfully insulting each other's sailing ability.

The only sounds were those of water flowing on either side of the sloop and splashing in the wake of their prow. The slow putt, putt, putt of the engine was hypnotic, lulling Amelia into the same pensive mood as Garth. He isolated himself at the bow, peering into the darkness.

Amelia kept her hand on the tiller, holding a course that hugged the shoreline. Jilly and Shelby stayed farther out, but almost parallel.

When they turned into the harbor and dropped anchor, Garth unloaded their gear quickly and silently. He stowed it in the trunk of his car. Amelia stopped beside him when she placed her cooler beside the picnic basket, and he slammed the back.

The air was heavy. It felt like one of Michigan's famous lake storms brewing. When Garth pulled onto the highway, the wind tangled Amelia's hair but cooled her face. She felt heavy, sodden, as if something was brewing between her and Garth, something explosive, potentially poisonous.

When he stopped at her house, she spoke what she'd been thinking, fueled by Frank's remark. "You're not in charge of the world, Garth. You can't assume responsibility for everything that happens and everyone around you."

"I'm sorry, Mel. I — I — just know that Buddy was right beside me. I could have grabbed him — or something."

"Garth, it *wasn't your fault*. It was an accident. I know this has reminded you of last year, brought back that pain. But — "

"Of course it has, Mel. What do you expect?" Garth leaned his head between his hands, white-knuckled on the steering wheel.

Amelia had seen Garth cry one other time in the years they'd known each other. It was when his old Lab, Nero, had died. The dog was thirteen years old, but so was Garth.

She pulled him into her arms and held him. She felt his tears soak into her shoulder, dampen her old cotton sweater. Some of the tears were for Reggie, she suspected, some for Buddy.

A part of her wanted to cry with him. But a part of her was still angry. At Garth. At Reggie. Yes, even at Buddy. And at someone else, whoever was determined to ruin all of their lives.

When Garth finally pulled away from her, he said, "I'm going to the hospital tomorrow, Mel, to see Buddy. Go with me."

"Sure. Call me when you get up. I can go any time."

The hospital in Muskegon was only about twenty-five miles away. It was an overcast, heavy day, matching their mood. The brilliance of Indian summer was coming to an end.

Amelia didn't know why she was surprised to find so many of their friends there. Stony Bay was a small community. Everyone knew everyone, and almost everyone was close.

Sandy, half-sat, half-lay in a chair in the reception room.

"Sandy, have you been here all night?" Amelia asked.

"I haven't been of any use to anyone, but I couldn't leave. I guess I look terrible." Sandy pushed at her hair as if Amelia's asking had made her aware of her appearance.

"How is Buddy?" asked Garth.

"Not great, Garth." Sandy shook her head. "His hands are burned the worst. He put them right into the center of the fire to catch himself. He has first-degree burns all over."

"He won't play football again," Garth predicted.

"Garth!" Amelia screamed. "What a thing to say."

"Is that all that matters to you?" Sandy had been saving her anger for someone. "Is that all anyone in Stony Bay can think of — football? Of course, he'll never play again. He'll do good to use his hands for *anything*." She fell back onto a dirty, orange Naugahyde couch, cratered with cigarette burns, and sobbed.

Garth, looking at no one, turned and ran toward the double doors at the end of the hall.

Amelia sat beside Sandy. "Garth didn't mean that, Sandy. He's — so upset. He — we all care about Buddy, Sandy. You know we care. You're tired. Why don't you go home with us when we leave?"

"I already told her I'd take her home." Jilly came up behind Amelia. Amelia didn't know why she was surprised to see Jilly, but she was. Maybe because she thought Jilly would stay as far away from hospitals and tragedy as she could for the rest of her life.

"Jilly has been wonderful," Sandy said. "She stayed right here with me and Buddy's parents all night."

"Oh." Now Amelia was the one put in a position of feeling guilty. She had gone straight to bed, and she hated to admit it, because she was exhausted, straight to sleep.

She turned, but Garth hadn't returned. Maybe he talked someone into letting him see Buddy. Her eyes rested on a tall, thin man leaning on the counter. "What is Travis Westerman doing here?"

"I called him," Jilly said. "I figured there was a story that needed to be written, since Stony Bay has lost *another* quarterback. Ironic, isn't it?"

"Maybe the position *is* jinxed. Like everyone's been saying." Sandy bit her lip, holding back another crying jag. It was obvious that was the way she'd spent part of the night.

"That's a word readers like." Travis walked into the conversation. "You think the team is jinxed?" Gray-blue eyes, expectant, stared from face-to-face. No one answered his question.

"It does seem ironic that Garth Dreyer was standing right beside someone who's the victim of a tragedy," Travis said. "And that Stony Bay has lost another quarterback. Maybe Garth has ambitions beyond our wildest dreams. Maybe he'll stop at nothing to get what he wants."

Amelia was on her feet instantly. "No! Take that back, Travis. It's not true!"

"Maybe Garth wants to be a star, like Reggie," said Jilly.

"I think there's a good story here," Travis said. "And I may be the only one who dares write this one."

"Don't you dare write anything that incriminates Garth in this accident, Travis Westerman!" Amelia exploded in all directions. Everyone here wanted to paint Garth as sinister as possible. They needed a scapegoat for another tragedy, and Garth, already tainted, just happened to be handy.

She clenched her fists, needing to hit out at someone. Before she said something she might be sorry for later, she ran. Turned and dashed out of the hospital waiting room, down the sterile hall, smelling of antiseptic.

She kept going to the car, collapsing in the front seat, crying, crying until there were no tears left. A few minutes later, Garth hurried out to the car and got in. He looked like someone who had just lost all hope. He never questioned Amelia's being in the car instead of in the waiting room. Starting the Chevy, he returned to the highway automatically.

Off in some place that Amelia didn't feel comfortable entering, he never said a word all the way back to Stony Bay.

But when he stopped at her house, he turned and stared at her, searching her eyes as if she had all the answers to all his questions.

"What? What is it, Garth? Did you see Buddy?"

"Yes. . . . For a short time, Mel. He's . . . he's in bad shape. While I was there . . ." Garth paused.

"What happened?" She grabbed his arm as if she could pull something from inside him that Garth didn't want to tell her.

"Buddy whispered. . . . He can hardly talk. His lungs were seared by the flames. All he could do was whisper. . . . I heard him, Mel. I heard what he said."

"What did Buddy tell you, Garth?" Amelia begged.

"He was pushed . . . someone *did* push him. He felt a strong, deliberate hand give him a shove."

Amelia couldn't speak. She waited, pains shooting through her chest.

"Mel, someone . . . someone tried to kill Buddy."

Chapter 9

Without wanting to remember them, Amelia thought of Travis's words. *Maybe Garth has ambitions beyond our wildest dreams.* Could that be true? Could Garth want to be quarterback so bad that he. . . . No, *no!*

The questions and her fear hung there, haunting Amelia all the rest of Sunday and all day Monday. Not seeing Garth or hearing from him during that time added to her concern. A combination of her own confusion, of the idea of someone standing to gain by Buddy's accident, allowed a tiny, niggling doubt to enter her mind. Her imagination fueled the idea, enlarged it.

Doubt was like a slow poison that oozed through her, destroying her trust.

On Monday at cheerleader practice, the doubt became a full-blown worry.

"Look," Jilly pointed to the field where the Bombers practiced. "Coach Pal has put Garth into the quarterback slot."

Amelia's hand clutched her megaphone until her knuckles were white and her fingers ached.

They leaned on the fence at the far end of the football field. Frank Evans trotted out for a long pass and fell, skidding on the wet grass near them, while catching the spiraling football.

"Frank, come here," Jilly called.

When Jilly called, guys obeyed as if under some spell she cast. Frank got to his feet and hurried to where the two girls stood. Amelia would have laughed at his appearance if she had been in the mood to laugh. His jersey was muddy, the number seven smeared so it was tarnished gold. His pants were wet and grass-stained. Under his eyes he wore dark smudges of Eye Black which made him look like a tired raccoon.

"Hey, sweet thing. Did that catch impress you?"

"You always impress me, Frankie. What's Garth doing at quarterback?" Jilly asked.

Frank glanced back upfield, admiration on

his face for the passes Garth heaved almost to the end zone.

"Coach Pal said it was either me or him. I didn't want that pressure. Garth said he'd try. Looks to me like he's going to be better than anyone dreamed — better even than Buddy. I don't know why Pal didn't think of giving him the place earlier."

"Maybe Garth didn't want it." Amelia expressed her hope.

"If he didn't, he's sure getting used to the idea in a hurry," Frank said. "I think he likes it. And he's a natural."

"Isn't he worried about that position being jinxed?" Shelby, looking almost as disheveled as Frank, joined the conversation.

"Who says that?" Frank frowned.

"It's the newest hot rumor." Shelby grinned. "You were smart to chicken out."

Giving Shelby a dirty look, but not bothering to correct his assumption, Frank spun around and launched the football back in Garth's direction.

Alan Hall was practicing kickoffs, and Frank dashed to pick off a high, tumbling ball.

"Is that really the word, Gumby?" Jilly

asked. "Or did you make it up just now for Frank's benefit?"

"I've heard it all day. Honest."

"Okay, people, if you aren't going to practice, we might as well go home." Ms. Carter, the cheerleading coach, reminded the squad of why they were on the field. "Let's have a three-layer pyramid with Jilly on top, somersaulting off at the end of the cheer."

Jilly groaned. "She's killing me today."

"Maybe I can pick up the pieces when you're finished." Shelby waved and walked back toward the school.

After another half hour, Carter gave up. She dismissed the squad with a shrug and a shake of her head. Everyone kept watching football practice instead of cheering.

"What did I tell you, Jilly?" Travis Westerman stopped Jilly and Amelia as they started to leave for home. He had been leaning on the fence watching the team, too. "Dreyer's dreams have come true. And strangely enough, he seems right for the job," he said sadly.

Amelia knew that grief did strange things to people. Could Travis not stand someone out there taking Reggie's place? Could he hate the idea so much, he'd see to it that *no one* filled Reggie's shoes?

Jilly stopped and put her arm around Travis. "He won't be as good as Reggie, Travis. No one ever will."

"A lot of good that does Reggie. But thanks for saying it, baby." Travis spoke to Jilly but stared at Amelia as if surprised to see her. He was the one who didn't belong here.

"Why are you hanging out here, Travis?" Amelia asked, although she realized he did have a legitimate reason. He *was* the sports page in the *Bay Daily*.

"Hey, this is news, kid. Today, my readers got the tragic story of Buddy Nichols. Tomorrow, a new, rising star makes the headlines. Don't you remember, in fall, football is king. Long live the king. We hope. I love the idea of the position of quarterback being jinxed. Maybe Reggie left a curse on the job. That'll be my lead." Smiling, he wrote himself a note.

Travis started for the opening in the fence around the football field. He obviously planned to interview the coach, maybe Garth, anyone who would talk to him.

"Come on, Amelia," Jilly said. "Shelby will

drop you off at your place first. Or do you plan to wait for Garth?"

Sometimes, last year, Amelia and Jilly had sat in the bleachers and watched football practice, waiting for the guys to finish. Coach never liked it, since he said the players were distracted, but walking off the field and to the locker-room door gave the girls a chance to spend a little time with Reggie and Garth.

Amelia made a quick decision. "I think I'll wait for Garth."

"Want me to wait with you?" Jilly offered.

"No. If you don't mind, Jilly. I need to talk to Garth alone."

Jilly looked a little hurt, more likely lonely. This all reminded her of last year's fun, her loss, the changes in her life this year. Amelia almost changed her mind. But if she didn't talk to Garth soon, she was going to burst with the terrible turmoil inside her. It was awful to be torn between her two best friends, but tonight Garth was going to come first.

Shelby put in another appearance. Like an actor waiting for a cue, he seemed to always be on the sidelines. "Jilly Bean, let's grab a burger and a flick before curfew. You have time?"

Jilly gave Amelia one last look that Amelia couldn't read. "Sure, Gumby. I have to go to my locker first." She turned, took Shelby's arm, and they walked away together.

Chapter 10

Amelia walked slowly toward the bleachers where she could sit and watch the rest of practice. She felt a little strange, doing this alone. Even funnier, realizing she carried a megaphone in one hand. She was in charge of equipment, but someone must have picked up the megaphones for her, forgetting hers. She climbed up several steps quietly, trying not to let Coach Pal see her, although there were always a few people watching practice.

Setting the megaphone beside her, she concentrated on watching Garth. Tall and muscular, he moved easily, gracefully, throwing the ball as if he'd always been quarterback. He seemed to have all the time he needed, either to get around the tackles, or to find a man in the open.

The Bombers had started Garth's sophomore year with a lot of new players, otherwise Garth might never have been placed on the team as a linesman. He wasn't really large enough for that position. Maybe he'd have liked being backup quarterback last year, but he was never one to want attention. Until now? her mind echoed. Until now?

"Yell at anyone through that thing and Pal will have your neck in a noose." Travis's voice from behind startled her. He stepped down and joined Amelia.

"I know. He wouldn't even like me to be here."

"Sometimes I wonder what I'm doing here." Travis's voice got serious. "Now that Reggie is gone. Maybe I'm staying for my parents. One more year for Reggie, Reggie's team. What do you think about the ghost, Amelia? Do you think Coach is behind it? That he planned it to get this team fired up?"

"I don't know." She didn't trust Travis.

"You'll have to admit it worked. The Bombers were amazing Friday night. They'd have never played that well if they hadn't had a *cause*."

She needed to talk to someone. Travis knew everything that she knew, maybe more. He might let something slip if she got him talking. "Travis, if Pal staged Reggie's appearance at the pep rally, why have it come out of the lake again last night? If he had the team fired up, why have Reggie make another appearance?"

"Jilly and Sandy told me about that. He has to *keep* them motivated. The Bombers win an important game like they did last week, and they relax. Get overconfident." Travis stared at the field while he talked.

"Are you saying that Reggie is going to show up every week?"

"Maybe not. A good coach has to be a good psychologist. Now Pal has Reggie and Buddy — one dead, one wounded." Travis's voice became sarcastic again. "This week they'll win for Buddy."

"He'll take advantage of the accident?" *If it was*, Amelia added to herself.

"Of course." Travis stood. "So will I. A story is a story. And this one is a reporter's dream."

"Travis, be serious about this. Someone is playing with our heads. Don't look at this as just another story. This is Reggie, your brother."

"Reggie would have loved it. You know, Mel, I think you've helped me find the right lead for tomorrow's headline. I was going to concentrate on discovering a star. On Dreyer being wasted as linesman, even as wide receiver this year, when he's obviously a splendid quarterback. But I didn't like thinking someone could take Reggie's place. Maybe I should listen to the rumor Shelby says is going around school — that the team, especially that position, is jinxed. I can have the whole town here Friday night to see if anything happens to Dreyer." Travis was thinking out loud, thinking things that Amelia didn't want spoken, much less happening.

"Travis — "

"Yeah that's it." He wasn't going to let Amelia interrupt. "Garth didn't *want* this position, didn't covet playing quarterback. I was on the wrong track. He *had* to take it. No one else wanted it. They were afraid of what might happen to them."

Amelia shivered. Was Travis planning a story or an actual event? Was he planning some accident for Garth to make sure the jinx, his story, continued?

"Reggie's revenge," he muttered under his breath, then laughed without humor. "Yeah, that's it."

"I — I have to go home, Travis." Amelia jumped to her feet, grabbed the megaphone, and stepped nimbly down the bleachers.

She ran all the way to the school, swinging

the door back, letting it slam behind her. Only when she was inside, did she stop to catch her breath.

She didn't want to think about any of this, the team being jinxed — no, the quarterback being jinxed. She especially didn't want to think about Garth being put in a vulnerable position. Would he really be in some danger because of it?

Of course not, she argued with herself as she headed for the storeroom in the gym.

Suddenly, when she got inside the huge, barnlike room, she realized how alone she was in the school. She stopped, listened, heard nothing. She scolded herself for being silly.

But this place was like a tomb. Her footsteps echoed across the polished hardwood surface.

Shadows hid the steel girders that framed the room. Without wanting to, she glanced around. That — that thing, posing as Reggie, had appeared out of nowhere twice before. Was it still around?

It wasn't real, she said over and over. There was no such thing as a ghost. But a person who meant some harm was just as scary. She felt eyes staring at her from every direction. Twice she whirled around. Nothing. No one.

A sense of evil surrounded her. It lurked in

the shadows, waiting. It glared from dark corners with cold yellow eyes. Amelia had only to invite it in, and it would whisper truths she didn't want to hear.

Fumbling with her key to the storeroom, she opened the door, tossed the megaphone into the shadows. She heard it thump and bump and roll.

Pressing her back to the door, she stared into the gloom that closed off all her escape routes. Her locker was in the front hall, between the door to the auditorium and the gym. Her purse, car keys, jacket were there. She had to have them.

Breathing deeply, she forced one foot, then another, across the polished gym floor. Through the double doors. Down the hall, her footsteps echoing. It took three tries to work her combination lock. Between each try she looked over her shoulder. Wasn't the custodian here someplace? Where was Ms. Wiggens? Principals were supposed to stay till everyone else had gone home, weren't they?

The locker hinges creaked. Her purse tumbled out onto the floor, but it didn't open and spill. She grabbed it, snatched her jacket, slammed the door, and clicked the lock shut.

Practically running, she hurried down the

hall, looking back just as she turned the corner. She slid, stumbled, splattered onto the floor, hitting hard and twisting her leg under her.

What? There was a puddle of water on the floor in front of the trophy case. Slowly she raised her head and looked at the glass. Nothing there except the display. The uniform, might as well have been the phantom, looming over her.

Her eyes swung back to the floor. A tangle of wet weeds twisted around her tennis shoes. The slimy surface had caused her to go out of control.

Almost robotlike she bent, dipped her fingers into the water, brought them to her nose. A fishy smell filled her nostrils. Lake water. As if the ghost had come here after melting back into the lake.

Choking back a scream, she kicked off the weeds. She jumped up and gathered her things. She dashed for the door and the parking lot.

The evil she had felt followed her, stretched curved talons toward her back, scraped across her shoulders.

"Go away!" She spun around, her hands flattened on the cold car door, fingers searching for the lock.

"Nothing is there, can't you see? Nothing, nothing, nothing!" She sobbed out the words, trying to convince herself.

With a shaking hand, she jammed her key into the slot, twisted it. She pushed the silver button, clutched the icy handle, yanked the door open. Inside the car, she pressed the master lock. But even the loud *click* did nothing to convince her that she was safe.

Chapter 11

She sat there, shivering, for a full minute. Then she said to herself, Your imagination is running overtime.

I didn't imagine the lake water in front of the case.

How long had it been there? All day? The custodian would have mopped it up. Maybe. He had a big building to keep clean. That door wasn't used as often as others.

Someone is trying to frighten me — us — who? Who was the target of this scare campaign? What did the — the ghost want?

It wants Garth, a voice inside her whispered. *Now it wants Garth.*

"Why?" she shouted and pounded the steering wheel. "What has Garth done to you?" *Become quarterback.*

She was being totally irrational. A puddle of water in the hall was making her crazy.

But once she had the idea in her head that Garth was in danger, she couldn't get it out. She took a notebook from the car door pocket, the one her mother used to keep gas and oil records. Ripping a sheet from the back, she scribbled a note.

> I NEED TO TALK TO YOU, GARTH.
> CALL ME THE MINUTE YOU GET
> HOME. AMELIA

She added the tiny word LOVE in between home and Amelia.

Before she could do any more thinking, she unlocked her door, slipped out, tucked the note under the windshield wiper on Garth's car, and ran back to her own car.

She drove straight home with her temples pounding and a voice saying over and over, *Garth. I want Garth. The quarterback is jinxed. He's in danger. You can't protect him, Mel.* Once, at a stoplight, she turned, looked in the seats behind her. "No!" she shouted.

She pulled into the driveway, ran for the house. Slammed the door behind her and leaned on it.

In the kitchen her mother was chopping tomatoes for a salad. "I haven't seen much of you lately, Amelia. Everything all right?"

"Of course. Why shouldn't it be?" Amelia snapped before she could stop herself.

Her mother looked at her. She didn't say a word, just stared.

"I'm sorry, Mom. I think I'm tired. I'll be right back down and help you fix dinner." Amelia left before her mother could say anything.

Upstairs, she dumped her books onto her bed. She stared at the phone as if she could make it ring. *Be home, Garth. Call me. Right now.* She glanced at her watch. He was probably still on the field or maybe in the shower. She'd try to be patient. She'd help her mother.

The kitchen was warm and spicy smelling from something in the oven. Amelia peeked at an apple pie, stirred a pot of lentil soup that had been on the back of the stove all day. She opened the cupboard, got out three plates, three soup bowls, three salad bowls, took them to the kitchen table.

"Dad will be ecstatic. His favorite meal." Her voice shook.

"It's his birthday, honey."

"Oh, no, I totally forgot. What's he going to think of me, Mom? What can I do?"

"Write him a note. He knows you're busy with school. And your own life. He'll forgive you, but a sweet note would help."

Plates clattered as Amelia set them down. Flatware chinked against them. She got out some cloth napkins and pulled them through rings, fluting the edges, laying them on the plates for a special dinner look.

"Are you sure everything is all right at school, Mel?" Her mother was too perceptive.

"Sure. Garth is going to be quarterback."

"That's nice. How is Jilly? I haven't seen her lately. I miss her coming over all the time."

"She's fine. She's been hanging out with some different people. I think she likes a guy from the drama department. But he wants her to drop cheerleading."

"Maybe she should. I'm sure it's hard for her to go to the games," Amelia's mother said.

"I guess I want things to stay the same."

"They're not the same, Amelia. Nothing will ever be the same for Jilly. You understand that. You've been a good friend to her through all this."

The phone rang.

"Will you answer, Mom? It's Garth. I'll talk to him upstairs. And I'll write a card for Dad before I come back down. I promise." Amelia ran out of the kitchen and to her room.

"Garth? Are you all right?" Amelia grabbed the phone.

"Of course I'm all right? Where'd you go? I thought you were waiting for me."

"I remembered I had Mom's car. Garth, when I walked back through the school, something odd happened." Amelia hesitated.

"Mel, what happened?"

"There was a pool of water in front of the trophy case, Garth, Reggie's case."

"So." He tried to make light of what she'd said, but his voice got quiet. "A dog got in the school."

"Garth, it was lake water. It had lake weeds in it. It looked as if — as if — well, as if Reggie had gone from the lake back into the case."

"Someone must have put it there deliberately. Did you see anyone? Did anyone see you going into the school?" Now Garth's voice held a note of worry.

"I — I felt really funny, Garth, as if someone were watching me, but no, I didn't see anyone." She wasn't going to tell Garth how scared she had been, how she'd totally freaked out.

He didn't say anything so she kept talking. "Seeing that uniform, Reggie's photo — well, I might as well have seen the ghost again. I'm scared, Garth, really scared. And I don't even know what to be scared of."

There was another long silence on Garth's part. Amelia waited him out. He was always so logical about everything, but she knew he wasn't going to find any logic about a ghost, about what was happening to them.

"Okay, Mel, someone is trying to scare you — me — the team, all of us. I don't know who or why, but we won't play this game. We won't be scared."

"But I *am* scared, Garth." Amelia's voice broke.

"Travis is trying to build up the idea of Bay's quarterback being jinxed. If I buy into that, Mel, I won't be able to play. None of us will," Garth said.

Garth is quarterback now. Garth is in danger.

"Can you come over after dinner, Garth? It would help me to talk," Amelia said. "To be with you."

"I need to study. If Coach is going to trust me in the quarterback slot, I can't let him down," Garth said. "I like the position. I think I might be good at it."

"I know you'll be good at it. I watched long

enough to see that. You have hidden talents."
She lowered her voice, teasing, trying to forget
her fear.

Then she said, "Garth, please come over.
Study here."

"I really can't, Mel. I'm sorry. We'll talk tomorrow." He hung up before she could protest
more.

She banged around finding her dad a card,
then tried to settle down. It wasn't right to
take her frustration out on her family. She was
writing her father a note when the phone rang
again. She jumped, then grabbed it before her
mom could answer.

"Did you call me back, Mel?" Garth's voice
sounded funny. It sent shivers all over her.

"No," she whispered. "You called me."

"You didn't call with the sound of water dripping in the background? Say nothing just to
give me a bad time?" His voice was tight.

"No, Garth."

"Okay, I'm unplugging the phone. I *have* to
study." He hung up.

"Fine, Garth, you study." Slowly she returned the receiver.

Immediately the telephone rang again, star-
tling her. Her hand hesitated over it, waiting

for it to ring again. It did. She grabbed it.

For a couple of seconds there was no sound, but no one hung up. Her hand tightened on the phone, started to sweat. *Swish, hush, swish-hush.* Water moving, waves.

"Who is this?" she whispered, unable to stay silent.

"Reeeeggggie." The voice was low, hoarse, barely a croak. "Beware of Friday's game."

Amelia slammed the receiver down. Before she could take a breath it rang again. She jerked it up. "Stop this!"

"Amelia? Is that you? It's Shelby."

"Shelby? You dialed my number *again*, didn't you?"

"Hey, don't bite my head off. I didn't call before. I need to talk to you about something important."

Was this a coincidence? Shelby's calling right after someone else? "What?"

"Amelia, I want you to let Jilly make her own decisions. If she wants to drop the cheer-leading squad, don't try to talk her out of it."

"Are you trying to stir up trouble, Shelby? Why are you calling everyone you know this evening?"

"What?" Silence, then: "For your information, Amelia, you're not everyone I know. But you *are* the person who has the most influence on Jilly. And you're the one who's helping her remember what she needs to forget."

"When did you become such an expert on Jilly, Shelby? I don't know why you're doing this, but keep in mind that Jilly is my best friend. And I'll do anything or say anything to her that I need to. You have no idea what she's been through this last year. You come along and on some whim — I can't imagine what — decide to try to change her life."

"Maybe you're a selfish best friend? Maybe it's you that can't handle the change. Jilly needs a change of scenery. She needs to hang out with someone besides dumb jocks. And I'm going to make sure she does. I should have known I couldn't have a reasonable conversation with you."

"At least you spoke to me this time. I'm on-to your games, Shelby. You aren't scaring anyone."

She slammed the phone down, sat staring at it, daring him to call back.

No one called again, but the damage had been done. Someone *had* been watching, waiting for her in the school. The same person had called Garth, then called her. Garth was going to pretend not to be scared, but she couldn't do that.

But it was Garth she was frightened for. Something was going to happen to Garth at Friday night's game.

Chapter 12

There was no time to be alone with Garth before Friday night's football game. After school he had practice, then he went straight home to study.

Only Amelia knew how tense he was. They both were pretending they hadn't received the mysterious phone calls. Neither mentioned it again.

Travis Westerman had followed through as promised with two articles. The first was about Buddy Nichols getting injured. The second was about the possibility of the Stony Bay Bombers being a jinxed team.

At the game Friday night there was a record turnout for a Bombers' game. Amelia wondered how many of the crowd were there because they were afraid they'd miss some catastrophe.

A tenseness in the air matched that inside

Amelia. All day long it had threatened to rain. The huge spotlights were surrounded with halos of vapor. The crowd waited, almost holding its collective breath, eyes focused on the dark tunnel where the Bombers would appear. What a perfect backdrop for Reggie's ghost to make an entrance. Would he dare?

Amelia stared into the gloom, gripping her megaphone, stomach tight, a bandlike vise around her forehead, making her temples pound.

A hand touched her shoulder. "Oh!" She swung around.

Jilly spoke as she turned. "You look worried, Mel. Have you talked yourself into believing Travis's article?"

"What do you mean, Jilly?" Amelia tried to keep her voice from shaking.

"You seem really tense. You and the whole crowd. I think they all came to see if Garth would get hurt, don't you?"

Jilly had said what Amelia was thinking.

"They're going to be disappointed," Amelia said, then motioned for the cheerleaders to bring the team out.

The crowd roared as the Bombers jogged onto the field. The captains watched the referee toss a coin. Crooked Valley won the toss and got the ball. Amelia watched Garth take a seat on the bench and pull a towel over his head. Was he worried? As tense as she felt?

Alan Hall kicked a high spiral toward the visiting team. One of their players caught the ball, ran it all the way up the field for a touchdown. Crooked Valley wasn't tense, scared, or intimidated by the Bombers.

"Well," said Jilly, smiling. "That breaks the ice."

Amelia was able to breathe. Maybe it relaxed the Bombers to be challenged from the first whistle. They played like champions the rest of the night. One touchdown. Two.

Amelia screamed until she was hoarse, then yelled some more. It helped. "Garth is about to throw for a third touchdown," she called to her squad. "Get ready to count the score." She ran back toward the bleachers.

She watched, her hands balled into fists as on their next possession Garth ran the ball into the end zone himself. She led another rousing cheer. Nothing bad was going to happen tonight. Garth wasn't going to let it happen. He was right. He couldn't be afraid and play well. Winning would dispel all the ghosts anyone could come up with.

The crowd changed their loyalty from Reggie Westerman. "Dreyer, Dreyer, Dreyer," they chanted. "Vader, Vader, Vader!" Fickle as always, they were in love with their new hero. In love with a team that kept coming back despite the odds.

With Garth hot, the Bombers wiped out Crooked Valley forty-eight to seven. Amelia breathed a sigh of relief when Coach Pal put in the second string for fourth quarter. Garth was safe.

He had thrown for three touchdowns besides the one he ran in himself. He was in such a good mood after the game, Amelia decided to enjoy it. They could have a serious talk later, if they needed to. Parents, students, total strangers came up to him at Dexter's and congratulated him on a game well played.

"This is almost embarrassing," he whispered to Amelia.

"Almost, but admit you love it," she teased.

"I didn't realize how great it is to be worshiped." He grinned at her.

Oh, Garth, you don't really mean that, do you? The icy fear she hoped was gone gripped her heart again, but for a different reason now. Garth turned his back to her. He became a distant stranger as he soaked up the praise, the hero worship, his new-found fame. He seemed to forget she was sitting next to him. It was almost as if he was becoming Reggie Westerman.

The next day, Coach had promised them a cookout at his lake home if they won, but it wasn't until four o'clock. Garth had said he wanted to go visit Buddy in the hospital before that. When Amelia went out to get in his car, she was surprised to find Frank driving, and Jilly in the front seat beside him.

"The team signed last night's football for Buddy," said Jilly. "They elected me to give it to him."

Amelia couldn't tell if Jilly was glad to be going or not. She seemed pretty cheerful. Then Amelia realized she was handling Jilly with velvet gloves again. She put Jilly's feelings and Shelby's strange phone call out of her mind. Jilly probably never knew he called her. It was his own idea.

She climbed into the backseat, but didn't sit close to Garth. He didn't seem to notice. He and Frank replayed the game over and over. Garth had kissed her goodnight last night. He hadn't noticed then, either, that she hadn't responded. He was all caught up in his new image. It seemed to Amelia that all he could think about, all he could talk about was his success. Of course, he never said "I." He wasn't as blatant as that. Yet. He said, "The Bombers this — the Bombers that — " until Amelia wanted to drop a bomb herself — in the backseat of the car.

After the hospital visit, where the doctors wouldn't let them stay long, they stopped for lunch at a Burger Bar on the outskirts of town. That was a mistake. And it didn't take long to discover their error. Apparently it was the hangout for Wolf Lake's football team. The Lakers were Stony Bay's worst rival, the school they had to beat to win in their division.

"Hey, Dreyer," shouted a guy twice the size of Garth. It was Ralph Dougherty, the linesman who'd delivered the fatal tackle to Reggie. "I hear the Bombers are having some problems this year."

"Yeah," another Laker said. "Your team is haunted and your players are jinxed. You're taking a big risk to play quarterback, aren't you, Dreyer?"

"Yo, man, how's Buddy Nichols? I'd be quaking in my boots if I was in your shoes, Dreyer." A tall guy in a green and white Lakers' jacket grinned like a Crest ad. "Two quarterbacks down, one to go."

"The Phantom Quarterback Killer strikes again." Dougherty jabbed the air with his fists. His friends encouraged him.

Amelia grabbed Jilly's arm. She was ready to punch out someone. They might have their problems at Stony Bay, but let an outsider attack, and they'd stand together.

"We'll see who's shaking when you get on the field against the Bombers," Jilly challenged. "You won't stand a chance."

"Well, maybe you'll have a few more little accidents before then," Dougherty said.

"You gonna be responsible for them, Dougherty?" Garth asked. "Maybe there's a good reason you've heard about our ghost. If we catch you in Bomber territory, you'd better make sure you have your bodyguards along."

"Come on, Garth. I've lost my appetite." Frank started for the door. "They have nothing but garbage in this place. Let's stop at Dexter's when we get back to the Bay."

Dougherty started for Frank, but his friends grabbed and held him. "We'll scramble your brains, Dreyer," he called after Garth. "Try to stay healthy until then, will you?"

"Do you think they could be behind the appearances of the phantom football player,

Garth?" Frank asked as soon as they got in the car and started for Stony Bay.

"It would take a lot of nerve for them to come onto our turf," Jilly said. "But remember, Mel, Ms. Hodgekiss said anyone could have come onto the stage from the back."

"How about the lake scene?" Amelia asked.

"Everyone knows where we have our beach bashes. That would have been even easier," Jilly said.

"I guess it wouldn't be too hard to get one of our uniforms," Garth said. "But Dougherty couldn't have been the one who pushed Buddy into the fire."

"Someone *pushed* Buddy?" Jilly asked.

"He said so. But he could have imagined it."

"We didn't know everyone there," Frank said. "The Lakers could have slipped someone into the party to do their dirty work."

"Maybe they didn't mean to hurt Buddy so badly," Jilly said.

"I — I think someone is using Reggie's uniform from the case in the hall." Amelia shuddered when she remembered the lake water and the weeds near the glass, the idea that someone was watching her. She had never told anyone but Garth, and she felt a bit foolish now for being so scared. She wished she'd have had the guts the other night to go find the school custodian, unlock the case, and check on the uniform. Easy to think of doing that now, though.

"They'd have to have a key to the trophy case." Jilly turned around and looked at Amelia. "Someone at the school would have to be helping the Lakers."

"I guess any number of nerds would do it for enough money," Frank said. "School spirit doesn't exist for some people."

"I just wish Reggie's ghost would show up again soon. We'll be ready for him, won't we, Evans?" Garth slapped Frank on the shoulder.

"Yeah, but I'll handle it. You're jinxed, Dreyer, remember?"

They all got quiet until they reached Stony Bay. Running into the Lakers had confused Amelia even more. She didn't know whether to worry about Garth's being responsible for what was happening to the Bombers or to worry about his getting hurt.

No one wanted to eat by the time they drove into Dexter's parking lot. They slid out of Frank's car.

"Aren't you going with Frank?" Amelia asked, when Jilly hurried away. She followed Jilly.

"Is that what you thought when you saw us together today?" Jilly's laugh turned into a sneer. "The more I'm around all these jocks, Mel, the more I appreciate Shelby. He can actually talk about something besides touchdown passes and point spreads. He's bringing me to the party after play rehearsal."

Amelia almost asked Jilly why she'd bother coming to Pal's party with Shelby. The only people who would be there would be football players and cheerleaders and their dates. And most of the conversation would be about football.

"I miss you, Jilly." Amelia wished they could sit down and have a long talk, but they'd had so little time together recently. "Want to sail tomorrow?"

"How about Garth?"

Amelia felt her face getting hot. "He has to work."

"So you have time for me."

"Jilly, even if Garth was off work, you could go with us on his boat."

"Sure I could. It would be like old times. Just you and Garth, me and memories of Reggie. Thanks, Mel, but Shelby and I are flying into Chicago with Dad. He has business, so we'll catch a movie and dinner."

Now Amelia felt a little jealous. She and Jilly used to do that a lot. It was fun to shop for school clothes or prom dresses in Chicago. There were so many choices.

"Okay, see you later this evening. Let's eat together. I could get to know Shelby better." Amelia tried.

"Sure." Jilly headed for her car.

Amelia returned to Frank's car to find Garth in the front seat, talking football plays with Frank. She shrugged and climbed into the back.

Frank dropped them off at the bay stores, so Garth could get his car and take Amelia home.

"You're awfully quiet," Garth said, grinding the motor three times before it coughed to a rumble.

"Wow, you noticed." Amelia looked out the window.

"Okay, what's wrong, Mel? You've been acting funny since I took you home last night."

He *had* noticed. That was some help. She might as well get this over with. "Garth, how badly did you want to be quarterback?"

"What do you mean? I never wanted it at all. No one wanted the job. We drew straws and I came up with the short one."

"You never, never last year or even the one before envied Reggie's popularity? Wished you were star of the team? Wondered if you could play his position just as well as he did?"

"Mel, what brought on that question? It doesn't sound like something you're saying off the top of your head."

Amelia stared at her hands, fingers long, nails neat, turned them over to find calluses from pulling the lines on a sail and the hint of walnut stain from helping her mother refinish a dresser a couple of weeks ago.

"There's some — gossip — I'd have to call it. Travis said . . ."

"What, Mel?" Garth's voice hardened.

"He didn't really mean that you caused Reggie to get hurt, or Buddy either — "

"Tell me, Mel. I want to hear this."

"Travis Westerman said that maybe you wanted to be quarterback badly enough to — to — help it along."

The silence in the car chilled her, made her wish she'd never brought this up.

"Is that what you think, Mel?"

"Of course not, Garth."

"But you've thought about it."

"I — I'm sorry. I couldn't help it. Once he said that, I couldn't forget it. I know better,

Garth, but — you've been so full of yourself, enjoying the glory so much that — "

Garth pulled onto the highway, throwing gravel behind him for six feet. It pinged against the hubcaps and rattled on the road. He was not a careless driver. He got no thrill from driving too fast, from being reckless. But the trip from the docks to her place frightened her. She didn't look at him, but she knew that would frighten her, too.

Chapter 13

They sat in front of her house, neither one moving, neither one saying anything. Finally she knew she had to mend this rift between them. Or it would fester. It would rot and destroy their relationship. And she loved him so much. She realized she had always loved Garth Dreyer.

"Someone wants us to fight, Garth. And to be afraid. I'm sure of it."

"Travis put the idea in your mind that I wanted to be quarterback enough to hurt Buddy. That wasn't your idea."

Amelia said, "I'd never have thought that, Garth. I love you. I know you. I know how good you are. And I know how you blame yourself for Reggie's death. You would never take advantage of someone else's pain."

"Pal said that if we were going to win, I had

to be quarterback. At first he said it was between me and Frank. But he said, in front of us both, that he thought I'd be better. Frank said so, too. He didn't want the job. He didn't think he could compete with Reggie's reputation. He thought I could handle that. Pal said we have to win this year. We have something to prove."

"Travis doesn't want to think the team can win without Reggie," Amelia said. "He's the one who said you'd do anything to be quarterback. I think he's behind all of this, Garth. The ghost of Reggie — just to remind us."

"Who pushed Buddy into the fire?"

"I don't know. Maybe no one pushed him deliberately. He imagined that. But read the articles Travis is writing, Garth. Half the articles are about Reggie. About how good he was. Travis compares everything you've done, the way you play to Reggie. He's not going to let Stony Bay forget his brother."

"Anyone you talk to on the team thinks Coach planned Reggie's ghost, Mel. And Coach has told us he'll lose his job if we don't win."

"That's not fair. Surely school officials won't fire him because the team loses a few games. Do you think it's true?"

"The fans are used to us winning."

"I mean, do you think Coach is using Reggie to keep you inspired?"

"He could be. I don't like thinking about it."

"Not thinking about it won't make it go away, Garth." Amelia kept being frustrated by Garth's avoidance of the subject. But she couldn't make him worry. She sighed. "I'll only be a minute, Garth. Will you wait for me?" She gave him a chance to say, I'm still angry. I want to go to this party alone.

"Of course." He pulled her back when she slid out. "I love you, Amelia. All of us are under a lot of pressure. We can't let it destroy us. We can't let someone who is angry and bitter destroy us."

Amelia had been to Joe Paladino's home before. But today, for the first time, she thought about how much it must have cost.

"How can a teacher afford this kind of place, Garth? Have you ever thought about that?"

Garth shrugged. "Coaches make pretty good money. And his wife teaches at the elementary school."

"He sure wouldn't want to lose this."

Five acres of pine, spruce, maple, and oak trees were finishing their fall show. The two-story colonial spread across half an acre. Porches wrapped around each story and a widow's walk topped it off like a wedding cake. Instead of a bride and groom, an expensive telescope and lounge chairs filled the roof-top deck.

The lake lapped the front two acres. A boathouse, dock, and two power boats hugged the shore. Two buoys helped designate a swimming area.

Paladino would lose a lot if he was fired as coach of the Stony Bay Bombers, Amelia realized. He'd told the players he had to win to keep his job. If that was true, how far would he go to make sure they kept winning? To bring in crowds to every game?

All this swept through Amelia's mind as she and Garth backed and maneuvered to find a place for his car. It looked as if everyone in school had been invited to this bash.

Garth got a grill and some charcoal from the back of the car. They didn't bother knocking at the front door. No one would be inside, unless changing to bathing suits, or using the bathrooms.

"Look, Garth." Amelia pointed.

There was a hand-printed sign on a tree at the corner of the house.

KILLERS,
YOU ARE ALL KILLERS.

As they followed the flagstone walk, nearly every tree held a sign.

WHO IS NEXT?
FOOTBALL SUCKS.
SOMEONE HAS TO PAY.

"What's going on?" Garth said to Frank, the first person they met.

"The people who came early helped Paladino clean up some of them. There were signs on his front door, on all the trees, on the grills, down at the boathouse, everywhere," Frank said.

A chill, not from the icy Coke Frank handed her, flew over Amelia.

Garth took his grill to the patio, poured charcoal into it, saturated the coals with lighter fluid. "Let's look around while this soaks in, Mel."

Frank was glad to show them more of the signs that Pal had left up for everyone to see. Someone had done a lot of work printing and pinning them up for the party. They decorated the grounds like paper lanterns or streamers, but the messages were not partylike. *And no ghost wrote them*, Amelia thought.

A huge *whomp* interrupted their tour. Screaming followed. Amelia and Garth dashed towards the chaos. The crowd parted so they could see one of the grills flame toward the darkening sky like some Olympic torch, out of control.

Mrs. Paladino rushed to her husband, as did several of the players.

"I'm all right. I'm fine," he said loudly. He tried to laugh. "But what happened?"

When Amelia and Garth got close, Amelia could smell the fumes that fed the blaze.

"It's gasoline, Pal." Garth grabbed the fire extinguisher from Mrs. Paladino, who had acted with as much cool as anyone there. He fizzed the foam on the grill, smothering the flames.

"Gasoline? I never — "

"Someone did," Garth said, his face dark with anger. "Someone doused *my* grill with gas."

"But why? Fortunately, I moved fast enough to get away, but *you* might have gotten burned if you hadn't walked away. Obviously, someone is trying to intimidate our team, and my new quarterback. Someone is hoping to sabotage our winning year. No one, you hear me, not one of you, is going to be successful." Coach Pal raised one arm and pointed around the crowd. "You aren't scaring me, and you aren't scaring my team."

This is scaring *me*, thought Amelia. She clutched Garth's arm, wishing she could lock him up, keep him safe until the football season was over. She wished she'd never heard of the deadly sport.

Chapter 14

The party continued, but all the players were angry. There was talk of, not so much who was doing the mischief, but of "We'll show *him*." If Coach, himself, had stirred up his players, or wanted them on edge, he must have been really happy.

Amelia tried to get away from the talk. She found Jilly and Shelby sitting on the rock wall that circled three sides of the patio.

"It's certainly not a boring party," she commented, feeling awkward, and hating feeling that way around her best friend.

Jilly laughed. "You can say that again."

"It's certainly not — "

They laughed and it broke the ice. Shelby got up, frowned at them, and went to get another drink.

"I think Shelby is bored," Amelia said.

"We're leaving early, Mel," Jilly said. "You

won't take it personally, will you? You seem to be taking everything I say or do lately personally. You don't like Shelby, do you?"

"I like him fine. He just doesn't fit in too well, and that makes it hard for things. . . ." She almost said, to be like they were.

Jilly knew it, and it made her stiffen. "I guess it can't be like it was, Mel."

They sat quietly, watching people, having run out of conversation. Amelia blanked her mind. Another possible accident — although avoided — haunted her.

Shrieks of laughter, yelling, hooting, fun interrupted their silence and Amelia's worry.

This time the commotion wasn't against the team or Coach Pal. The football players, angry about the signs and the near accident for Pal, needed to vent their anger on someone. Shelby Gunderson happened to be handy, to make himself visible at the wrong time.

Since he was small, it didn't take four guys to pick him up and stuff him into the oversized trash barrel behind the patio. But four guys *wanted* to do it.

Jilly and Amelia moved toward the noise at the same time, but Amelia stopped, covered her mouth to hide a smile. Jilly kept going.

"You big bullies! Leave him alone." She ran to the bin.

"Come to his rescue, Jilly Bean?"

They left, laughing. It took both Jilly and Amelia to tug Shelby up and over the side and onto his feet.

He slammed one fist into the bin, swinging around and clutching the top, knuckles white, face bright red.

"Shelby, it's all right — "

"It's not all right, Amelia. Those damn jocks think they're so cool, so macho. I'll — I'll — " Shelby didn't finish saying what he wanted to do to get revenge. Maybe he couldn't think of anything, since he would certainly be at a disadvantage if he tried anything now. There were twenty-five of them, all gone back to pigging out and roaring with laughter. For them the fun was over. They felt considerably better to have found a convenient victim.

"I'll get even with them. I'll think of something." Shelby tried to brush coffee grounds from his white T-shirt.

Shelby? Amelia stared at him. Had he already been getting even? She remembered how he was suddenly in the hall after Reggie's first appearance. How he seemed to jump into the lake after Reggie's ghost, then come back out. Maybe he had been in the lake a few minutes earlier.

But the ghost was much bigger than Shelby.

Travis? Coach? Maybe she had been thinking along the wrong lines. Shelby hated "jocks" as he called everyone in sports. Now he was making threats and was partly justified.

"I'd like to leave now, Shelby," Jilly said quietly.

"That's good, Jill." Shelby took her arm. "I don't know why I let you talk me into coming. Hanging out with bovine mentalities was never my idea of a good time."

"I'm sorry, Shelby." Amelia tried to apologize for the whole crowd.

"It's not your problem, Amelia. Don't try to take up for these goons." Shelby took several deep breaths, as if trying to control his anger.

"What happened?" Garth chose the wrong moment to reappear on the scene.

"You missed it, Dreyer?" Shelby's eyes met Garth's. "What a shame. Maybe the sight of misplaced aggression would have inspired you next Friday, got your adrenaline roaring. I'm sure some of your buddies will be glad to fill you in on the details." He pushed Jilly toward the driveway.

Amelia stood watching them leave, then turned to Garth. "Some of the guys stuffed Shelby into the trash can."

Garth smiled. "Oh. I can see why he isn't a happy camper. Why does Jilly insist on bringing him to a party like this, anyway?"

"Because he's different. I think she's flaunting Shelby Gunderson in front of us."

"Fog's coming in," squealed Diane Hardy, behind them. "Let's hide."

The latest fad in Stony Bay was playing kid games, but especially what they called reverse hide-and-seek.

Garth pushed Amelia away from him. "Mel's it." He ran and was immediately gobbled up by the misty cloud that had sailed off the lake and lowered quickly around the party.

Amelia felt frustrated. Garth had completely ignored, or chosen to forget, the grill incident. But she'd try to be a good sport. She hated being "it." Her job was to find one other person, but instead of running and counting them in, "One, two, three for Garth," she would hide with that person.

Two looked for another and so on until all but one person were hiding in the same place. It was akin to how many people can you put in a phone booth or a Volkswagen bug. The wiggling, giggling pile of bodies usually made so much noise they were easy for the last, lone person to find.

Gravel crunched under Amelia's feet as she crossed the driveway. She walked reluctantly toward the woods behind the house. In seconds she lost the party noise of the patio — adult chaperons talking, glasses clinking.

The fog muffled all sound, surrounding it in misty cotton wisps. Her Nikes padded softly across pine needles, then crunched into a fall of maple leaves around a tree whose arms reached for her, black and bare against the dim grayness.

Waves of lake water whispered as she walked deeper into the trees. Gradually she lost all sense of direction. Was she moving deeper into the woods or back toward town? Why hadn't she found anyone yet?

A stick snapped. She whirled around. Nothing. Without meaning to, without wanting to, her memory replayed the image of Reggie rising from the lake. She turned round and round and round. *Please don't let me see the ghost. Don't let it make an appearance here.*

Her heart raced until she felt her pulse throb in her throat. The mist clogged every pore, filled her nose, choked her. Once more she spun around, peering into the gloomy haze.

Suddenly a shadow loomed ahead, moving toward her.

No, no! Oh, please, no!

Chapter 15

"Amelia?"

She sucked in a scream. "Garth, is that you?" She burst into tears.

He grabbed her and held her close. "Mel, what's wrong? For a minute he stroked her hair, then he pushed her away. "You scared yourself, didn't you?" He laughed softly.

She tried to stop crying. "No!" she said between sobs. "You scared me."

"I'm sorry. I was looking for you, hoping I'd find you before you found someone else."

Her fear progressed through anger to embarrassment. "It was the fog. It was so quiet. Can we go home, Garth? All of a sudden, I'm really tired."

"Okay. Let's stop and thank Coach."

Coach Paladino and his wife were on the patio. "Leaving early, Dreyer?" Pal asked. "This is the only night training hours are relaxed. Better take advantage of it."

"Amelia's tired."

"It was a great party," Amelia said, apologizing. "I'm sorry someone tried to spoil it."

"No harm done. We'll forget it until Friday. Then I'll remind the guys, so they can get angry again." Pal laughed, raising dark eyebrows.

"Coach, who — "

He didn't let Amelia finish her question. "Oh, I've had kids do fool things before. Someone thinks he's being cute. Might even be one of my players. I step on a lot of egos."

Coach Paladino didn't seem to be taking the signs or the near accident of the grill seriously enough to suit Amelia. Unless he knew who did it. Her mind returned to Pal being behind all the incidents that served to anger his players, get them revved up to win. If Paladino knew there was gas on that grill, he could be prepared to move fast enough to get out of the way of the flames. He could have pinned the signs everywhere before the party started, then staged the grill fire. It didn't seem like an adult thing to do, but she had seen adults act childishly before. If they had a good enough reason.

She told Garth her thoughts as they drove slowly through the fog to town and then cut east to her house.

"What do you think, Garth. Is he that desperate to win?"

"I don't know. He doesn't *need* to be, Mel. We really do have as good a team as we did last year. Maybe better. Pal is probably right. Someone had his feelings hurt. Maybe even a guy who tried out for the team and got cut at the end."

"But why use Reggie like he has?"

"Why not? He just thought that a ghost would be scary or dramatic, get everyone's attention. Notes or hate letters didn't seem to be enough. Maybe he's seen something like that on TV."

On Friday night, during the third quarter, she remembered.

No one was even close to Frank Evans when he staggered across the field, crumpled up, and passed out. Both teams were standing around waiting for the referees to argue with Pal over some infraction. It was picky on Coach's part. Probably a ploy to let his players rest a minute. They'd played hard to get one touchdown ahead of the Graycliff Groundhogs. The Groundhogs were in last place, so they played over their heads. They had nothing to lose and everything to gain by upsetting the Bombers.

"Frank's down!" Amelia grabbed Jilly's arm. "What's wrong with him?"

"Evans is our best receiver." Travis Westerman stood on the sidelines with the cheerleaders.

"Half the school has the flu," Amelia said. "It's probably flu." *Please let it be the flu.*

"Probably." Jilly stared at her black and white saddle shoes, then pulled up one gold sock, rearranging it so it crumpled into even ridges.

People got way too quiet for a football game. The capacity crowd in the stands seemed to be holding its breath.

There was no announcement. Nothing. A rookie player took Frank's place and the game resumed. What was one player down? There was always another to take his place.

"Go find out about Frank, Travis," Amelia said. "I want to know what happened to him." Travis had hung out near the cheerleaders the whole game, making Amelia nervous. She'd be glad to get rid of him.

"I will. This is going to make the game even better. My readers will want to know how the

Bombers overcame another obstacle. Or didn't." Travis grinned and left, walking down the fence boundary and toward the Bombers' bench.

Amelia paced the sidelines, waiting for an announcement or for Travis to come back.

Who came was Shelby. "The jinx strikes again, huh?" He didn't grin, but his tone of voice was sarcastic, pleased. "Someone is finally going to realize it isn't safe to play football in this town." Now he laughed and sat by Jilly on the bottom bleacher reserved for cheerleaders. For someone who hated football and jocks, Shelby wasn't missing a game this year.

The ambulance that was always present during games sped away, but without the siren screaming, without the lights flashing. If it was an emergency, they'd want to hurry, wouldn't they?

The game finished. Still no news.

One by one the guys came out of the locker room looking glum, even though the Bombers had won the game.

"What?" Amelia begged for information. "What happened?"

Each person she asked shrugged and hurried past her.

The Groundhogs left, looking just as disturbed. They had played the rest of the game as if they were more upset by Frank's leaving the game than the Bombers were. Or maybe the idea of winning got to them. They went to pieces at the end, letting Stony Bay get one more touchdown for good measure. Garth ran that one in himself instead of passing to the rookie who took Frank's place.

Finally Garth appeared, his face grim. Amelia ran to him, fell into step beside him. He was silent and withdrawn.

"Garth, say something!" she said finally. "Is Frank all right? Does he have the flu? What happened?"

"What happened, Mel, is that Frank was poisoned."

"Poisoned? How? Is he all right — or is he — " She couldn't say "dead." Frank couldn't be dead, could he?

"They think he'll recover. But he's really sick. No one would have known if one of the doctors hadn't been alert. And if he hadn't looked so bad that they raced him away still wearing his uniform. There were scratches on his back and shoulders. Dr. Blanchette noticed them and got curious."

"Garth, what are you saying? His *uniform* poisoned him?" Amelia wanted to shake the story out of Garth. She clutched his arm and stopped his race to the car. "Tell me."

"I'm trying." Garth's voice was shaky. "Someone had stuck pins in his shoulder pads. The pins had been dipped in some kind of contact poison."

"Contact poison," Amelia said slowly. "You mean if it touches your skin it can poison you?"

"The pins made scratches, helping the poison enter the bloodstream." Garth hesitated. "They have to run some tests, but by the condition of the skin, redness, scaling, and cracking, the doctor suspects benzene. Frank's other symptoms match, too. The poison affects the nervous system. That made him dizzy and nauseous. We all thought he had the flu."

"Who? Why?" Amelia's mind raced. "Why Frank?" *Instead of you*, her mind added quickly. "Instead of the quarterback."

She didn't realize she'd said the last words aloud until Garth spun her around, gripped her arms painfully.

"Mel — that poison was *meant* for the quarterback. Those weren't Frank's shoulder pads. They were mine."

Chapter 16

Amelia, in a frightened daze, followed Garth to the parking lot. Her mind remained numb, frozen, until she spotted a familiar figure. She grabbed Garth's arm. "Look, Garth, Travis is still here."

Travis Westerman sat in his car, driver's door open, one leg sprawled out. He was scribbling madly on a tablet by the dim overhead light. His face was covered with a grin that gave them no doubt that he was enjoying himself.

Amelia couldn't stand it. Her fear turned to anger. Before Garth could stop her, she stomped over to him.

"You have your headline, don't you, Travis?" She jerked the car door all the way open. "The team really is jinxed. Another player goes down. Which lead will you use?"

Travis looked startled, but then he smiled

again. "It's the truth as I see it. My readers want to read it. This is my job, so cool off, Mel."

"Now wait a minute, Westerman — " Garth didn't like the way Travis was talking to Mel.

"Tell her, Garth, tell her the facts of life. Was Evans drunk? Hung over? Tell her someone needs to take the responsibility for telling a player he's benched. Paladino sure won't. All he cares about is winning. You're the captain of the team. Maybe you should have told Frank Evans he was in no shape to play. You could have stopped Reggie and you didn't. This was your chance to redeem yourself."

"Wait a minute, Travis," Amelia said. "You don't have the whole story. Frank Evans wasn't sick or drunk. He was poisoned. He could die, and here you are thinking only about your story."

"Poisoned?" Travis ripped off the sheet he'd been writing on and crumpled it into a tight ball. "No wonder no one would talk to me. I thought — "

"You don't think, Travis. That's one of your problems. You don't think about people, only getting a story." Amelia let out the anger she'd been holding onto since Garth told her about Frank. It was mixed with fear and a terrible sick feeling, but anger was all she could express now.

For once Travis had nothing to say back to her. Then the rest of what he'd said registered with her — about Garth keeping Reggie from playing.

"Garth, what does Travis mean, you should have stopped Reggie from going on the field when — when — " Amelia turned back to Garth.

Garth sighed and leaned against the front fender of Travis's car. He closed his eyes and let his head roll forward.

"Last year, when Reggie got hurt — "

"When Reggie got killed, Garth." Travis sprang to his feet. In one swift movement he stood before Garth. "Don't mince words."

"When Reggie got killed. Reggie should never have played that game, Mel. He was hung over. Slow — he was so slow. I tried. I tried to protect him." Garth spun around and leaned over the car. Sobs racked his body.

Amelia stared at him, frozen, unable to move, to touch him. But her mind wasn't as much on Garth as what he had said. Reggie, hung over, should never have played that fatal last game?

"You could have stopped him, Dreyer. Somehow, you should have kept him off that field. He wasn't just hung over, he must have been drinking before the game." Travis's voice held anger and unshed tears.

"It was the pressure . . . the pressure. He said a couple of drinks would help him. He said if he was relaxed, he'd play better."

Travis grabbed Garth, twisted him around, then gathered the front of his jacket into his fist and pulled Garth close. "Tell the truth, Dreyer. I have to know. Did Paladino know it? Did he know what shape Reggie was in?"

"No." Garth shook his head back and forth, back and forth. "No, no, no. We protected Reggie. We kept him away from Pal. I — I don't think Pal would have let him play."

"But you're not sure, are you?"

"We hoped Reggie would be all right. At first he seemed to be in control. Once he got on the field, into the game, he was usually okay. But he was always scared. He talked big, but he was scared. Coach is adamant about no drugs, no alcohol, no steroids. He would have canned Reggie so quick — I think."

"You could have told Paladino, Dreyer. You didn't have the guts. You're smarter than Reggie, and a hell of a lot more responsible. I'll always think you could have stopped that tragedy." Travis got back in his car and slammed the door. Throwing the T-bird in gear, he screeched backward, swung around, and screamed out of the parking lot.

Amelia stared at the sports car's taillights until they disappeared.

She had loved football season, loved the game, loved cheering the players on and on until they won. That love was crumbling quickly, at finding out what went on behind the scenes, in the locker room, inside the players.

But right now she couldn't dwell on what had happened last year. She needed to worry about Garth.

"Someone is trying to hurt *you*, Garth. Not the team, but you." She said it out loud. "Travis hates you. He holds you responsible for Reggie's death. Maybe he — "

"I don't want to think that, Mel."

"If you don't want to think it's Travis, then who *do* you want to suspect? You said those were your shoulder pads tonight, the ones Frank wore by mistake. How could that happen?"

"Easy. Sometimes we throw them down when we're getting dressed. They all look alike, except for size, and Frank and I are about the same build. But I don't think anyone is after me."

"Garth, those were *your* pads."

"They didn't have my name on them."

"Were they in your locker?"

"Sure."

"You took *your* grill to the party. You were supposed to light it. Coach just happened to do it for you."

"They were trying to get it going in a hurry. A lot of people pour gas or too much lighter fluid on a grill. It's stupid, but they do it."

"But *you* didn't do it. Someone else did and conveniently forgot to tell you, thinking you'd light it. You were supposed to get hurt then, and when you didn't, someone tried again tonight, Garth. Think about it, Garth!" Amelia got into Garth's car and slammed the door.

"Okay, I'll think about it," Garth said, getting in beside her. "But I can't worry about getting hurt when I'm supposed to be playing the game."

"The game, the game, damn the game. Take me home, Garth. You can go to the hospital if you like, but I want to go home."

Chapter 17

They got word that Frank Evans would recover — slowly.

He was replaced. There were still a few eager players left on the bench who didn't believe the team was jinxed. Friday, the Bombers would travel to Wolf Park for a night game.

Garth and Amelia stopped talking about football. But then there was that inevitable next game.

A few of the players, some of the cheerleaders, and the band drove to away games. Most rode the two school buses designated to transport everyone. Neither Coach nor any school officials were tight on rules about how to get to the game. Just that everyone get there on time.

"I think Garth is driving, Jilly," Amelia said at lunch on Thursday. "Go with us."

Last year Garth and Amelia, Jilly and Reggie rode in either Garth's or Reggie's car. Thinking back, Amelia remembered that it was usually Garth who drove. Now she realized what she hadn't known then — Reggie was drinking, or wanted to drink. And even he would have respected the school's policy about drinking and driving. Two years ago, after a tragic accident, the whole student body took a pledge, "I won't drive while drinking. I won't ride with anyone who's been drinking."

"Jilly," Amelia asked, looking right at Jilly. "Did you know that Reggie was drinking a lot last year?"

Jilly stared at the dwindling cafeteria line. "Reggie liked a beer occasionally. Said it relaxed him. I wouldn't call that drinking a lot."

"Did you know he was half-drunk when he got hurt?"

Jilly stared at her plate of nibbled and mangled food. "If he was, why didn't Garth keep him from playing?"

"Why does everyone think Garth should have been Reggie's guardian? Jilly, someone is trying to hurt Garth. And I'm going to find out who it is."

"Tell someone. Tell Coach Pal. Tell the police."

"There wasn't any evidence, until the poisoning. The sheriff *is* looking into that. Worse, I can't get Garth to be scared."

"Garth isn't scared?" Jilly seemed surprised. "Garth is stronger than Reggie. Reggie was scared about a lot of things. But no one is perfect. People do things they don't really mean to do, or even want to do. Reggie just wanted to keep playing football."

Jilly collapsed back onto the bench and started crying. Amelia felt really frustrated.

"I'm sorry I upset you, Jilly. We'll plan on your riding with us tomorrow. We're leaving right after lunch."

"I — I — may go with Shelby. If he can get away. If he can't, I'll go with you, but don't wait for me."

The sky was gloomy, overcast, by noon on Friday. The air was heavy, rain-laden. It was going to be a miserable night if the storm moved in and the Bombers had to play in the rain.

Highway 20 took them due east through the national forest. Clouds had lowered until visibility was only about fifty feet. Amelia felt they were driving through thick cobwebs, woven between the dark trees that stood sentinel on either side of the road. Long, dark tunnels of trees that made her feel trapped, claustropho-bic. This was nightmare country with a deep, dark hole waiting for them at the end of the road. Each football game was now something to be endured, to survive.

"I hope this fog lifts before evening," Garth said, peering ahead. "Visibility will be nil after dark."

Amelia felt she had to help Garth drive. She stared ahead, mostly looking for deer. Often, if they heard a car, they stopped right in the middle of the road, frozen.

A couple of small towns relieved the feeling of isolation, but after White Cloud, the fog swirled thicker.

"I wondered why they called that town White Cloud," said Garth, trying to get Amelia to relax. She didn't buy it.

"The coaches should have called this game off."

"Are you kidding?" Garth grimaced. "This is our easy win. I'll probably play first quarter and get benched."

Please let that be true, Amelia thought.

When they finally got to Wolf Park, Coach made the players eat together at a local steak and potato café. Amelia looked around for Jilly.

She hadn't showed up at the car, so they didn't wait for her.

"Was Jilly on the school bus?" Amelia stopped Billy Rollins, who was in the band.

"I didn't see her. But I jumped on at the last minute. She may have been in the back."

A tuba player said he thought Jilly was helping lead cheers in the back of the bus on the way over. But he hadn't seen her since. People had scattered to look for food and bathrooms as soon as they reached the Wolf Park stadium.

Almost everyone headed for McDonald's. Amelia found Jilly there, in a booth with five other cheerleaders.

"There you are. Didn't Shelby come?"

"He had play practice. Squeeze in. I'm starving." Jilly was in a considerably better mood than at lunch.

"I guess so. You didn't eat lunch." Amelia walked away to order, not wanting to say anything else.

They laughed and talked about winning while they scarfed down Big Macs, fries, cherry pies, and double Cokes. They even laughed when someone wondered if the jinx went to away games. Amelia didn't think anything was the least bit funny, but she tried not to get angry. No one wanted to worry about the game.

"Oh, I ate too much. I'll never be able to get off the ground. I bet Carter will want a dozen flips and cartwheels right off." Jilly groaned.

Everyone groaned. "No barfing in front of a rival team," Amelia announced, trying to keep her own worries hidden. She and Jilly held out their hands for a slap from the rest of the squad to seal the pact. Then, arm in arm, they headed for the game.

Did the jinx go to "away" games? The phrase echoed over and over in her mind.

Shaking her head to clear it, Amelia put her mind solidly on tonight, this minute, this cheer, this game. The game wasn't very exciting, in fact, it was borderline boring. The Wolves weren't much competition for the Bombers. Most of their team were freshmen, and they couldn't do anything right. Amelia relaxed considerably when Pal put in the second string for some experience.

Garth waved at her once, and she waved back. Did he know she was nervous? Probably not. He was thinking about her, and when he spotted her, he let her know it. She felt warm, despite the misty evening, and her tenseness.

It had rained while they were eating dinner,

then slacked off to a drizzle for the rest of the night. The players were so muddy, Amelia wondered how they knew who was on which team once they broke formation.

The final buzzer was a relief. Finally, one game played without anything happening, without anyone getting hurt. She grabbed her coat. "Ride back with us, Jilly?"

"No, a bunch of us are going to play charades on the way back. Gumby's friends play it. It's fun." Jilly grabbed Debby Rollins's arm, and they took off running.

Amelia watched them go with a stab of jealousy. She headed for Garth's car.

"Are we really by ourselves?" Garth asked when he had changed and found her.

Amelia yawned. She'd wrapped herself in a blanket and napped while she waited for Garth. "I guess so. Jilly went off with Debby."

"Thanks, Jilly." Garth said, leaning over to kiss Amelia. "Remind me to tell her that in person tomorrow."

"I will," Amelia said, when Garth let her go, reluctantly.

He pulled out in front of the second bus, mostly players and cheerleaders. The band had left immediately.

"Don't drive too fast, Dreyer." Coach

stopped and pecked on the window until Garth rolled it down. "It's going to be hell to get home. But you guys were great. Thanks again for the win."

"He's in a good mood," Amelia said when Pal left.

"He should be. We got through this game with everyone in one piece. We're sure of the next two games. Then all we have to do is beat the Lakers and we've won the district again."

Amelia dozed off a couple of times. Garth kept the car creeping along at about twenty miles per hour. With darkness, visibility at any distance was pretty much gone. If there was going to be fog anyplace in the county, it was on this narrow forest road. Looking back, she could just barely see the headlights of the bus. If anyone was ahead of them, she hoped they wouldn't stop suddenly.

Just as that thought crossed her mind, a light filled the road, glowing like a huge, fuzzy sun.

"Look out, Garth!" she shouted. "Stop!"

Garth saw the light at the same time Amelia did. Fog turned into pale gold moisture. Like a streak of cold moonlight, the spotlight across the highway outlined Reggie's ghost, surrounding the phantom football player in a surreal glow. The number nine blazed like an icy

fire on his chest. One hand was raised, signaling
Garth to stop. The other pointed to their car.
Reggie's glowing helmet turned back and forth,
while hollow, dark eye sockets stared vacantly.

Instead of stopping, Garth swerved right,
trying not to hit Reggie. Driving onto the
muddy shoulder, even with no speed, was
enough to make them skid. In slow motion, it
seemed at the time, the car slid, spun around,
took flight, and rolled.

Chapter 18

When Amelia came to, she was hanging upside-down by her seat belt. Her first thought, though, was Garth.

"Garth, Garth, are you all right? Garth?"

He groaned — a good sign. "Mel, what happened?" He couldn't remember?

She pushed and pounded at her buckle until it released, making her tumble to the top of the car, which was now the bottom. The car rocked with her movement. It was like a huge beetle on its back, but she didn't think it would go far, just wobble. The car headlights shone into the cottony fog, cutting twin paths into deep forest.

Carefully she crawled to Garth. "Can you move, Garth? Does anything hurt?"

"Are you kidding. Everything hurts. I feel like I've been tumbled in a dryer."

She stopped holding her breath. Garth was all right.

"Reggie — it was that damn thing, that ghost, wasn't it? I remember now," Garth said. "Some fool was standing in the middle of the road. Who was that, Mel? Who was it?" He started fumbling with the strap around his waist.

Someone pounded on the window. The fog was so thick, the world looked smoky white. She could see only fists.

Voices reached them. "Dreyer! Amelia! Are you all right?"

Garth dropped on his shoulder and winced. He pulled on the door handle. "I think my door is jammed. Try yours."

"Garth, what are we going to tell people? If no one else saw — saw — Reggie, should we say we did?"

"The police won't believe us. They're serious about what happened to Frank, but they think the ghost is a school prank. Something for school authorities to handle. And they might say I was using that as an excuse for careless driving."

"Let's say it was a deer until we think it over," Amelia suggested. "Everyone will believe a deer."

Garth agreed and Amelia turned to her door again. It popped and flew wide as if it always opened upside-down. Hands reached inside to pull them out.

"What happened?" Debby Rollins asked. "Did you spook a deer?"

Bless you, Debby, Amelia thought. "Yes, it stepped right in front of us. There was no way to stop, so Garth swerved."

"Mel!" Jilly grabbed her arm. "Are you all right? What happened?"

"We're not hurt. We were lucky." Amelia took Garth's hand. There was a moment of deadly silence. Hazy, shimmering faces surrounded Amelia, faces that peered out of the fog at them like spirits with dark shrouds for bodies. She shook her head, feeling dizzy. Didn't they believe her?

"Hey, tough luck about your car, Dreyer." Will broke the spell everyone seemed to be under.

"Okay, okay people, show's over." Coach Pal shooed the crowd toward the highway. "What happened, Dreyer?" he asked. "Are you two all right?" He came closer to see for himself.

"We're fine, Coach." Garth explained. "A few bruises. Should we call the Highway Patrol?"

"We'll have to go on into White Cloud to call," said Pal. "One car accident, no one hurt. Maybe they'll let us come back out here tomorrow to make a report. Okay with you, Garth? Are you sure neither you nor Amelia is hurt?"

"We're sure. I just want to lie down someplace soft for about twelve hours."

It was a pretty somber group that piled back on the school bus.

"I'll ride with Coach," Garth whispered, touching Amelia's arm before she got on.

"Okay." Was Garth going to tell Pal the truth? What difference would it make? They couldn't take off through the woods, looking for someone — something — that had already disappeared.

Amelia looked around. "Jilly, coming?" Everyone was a dark blob in the fog, but Jilly stood by the door watching them load.

"Yeah, sure." She walked up the steps and flopped down by Amelia in the first seat. "You scared me, Mel. Are you sure you're all right? Maybe you should go to the hospital, you and Garth both."

"Maybe we'll go tomorrow," Amelia said. "I think you're supposed to — in case anything develops later."

The school bus engine roared, doors whooshed shut. It crawled on down the highway. Everyone got quiet, as if thinking about the wreck. Or maybe they'd used the rest of their energy being scared for Garth and Amelia and now were ready to zone out.

"What happened, Mel?" Jilly asked. "Garth saw a deer, is that right?"

"One minute we were creeping along, the next we were rolling, Jilly. Thank goodness we were going so slow."

Amelia didn't want Jilly to know they'd seen the ghost again. It would only upset her. And more publicity would renew the gossip and speculation at the school about who was pulling the prank. They might tell the police tomorrow.

It was hard to think of it as a prank now that the ghost's appearance in the middle of the road had caused an accident. She and Garth could have been hurt, badly. But if the phantom player wanted attention, if that was behind the appearances, keeping this visit secret should frustrate him. He'd have to show up again. And the more often he did, the more chances someone would have of catching him.

"What are you thinking, Mel? You're so quiet." Jilly took her hand.

"It could have been the bus, Jilly. I'm just glad the bus wasn't wrecked. Especially since we aren't hurt. If the — the deer had stepped in front of the bus — well, I don't want to think about it anymore."

"It must have been really scary."

"It was."

This appearance of the ghost wasn't planned to boost school spirits. Or get the team to "Win for Reggie." Tonight's game was over and the Bombers had won. It wasn't planned for spooky entertainment at the beach bash.

It was another attempt to hurt Garth. The ghost had stepped in front of Garth's car deliberately to cause a wreck. A wreck that could have killed both Garth and Amelia.

Someone must be really frustrated that his plans for Garth weren't working out. He had failed twice — well, three times if you counted the grill fire. The attempts were coming closer and closer together. Amelia felt absolutely certain that the killer wouldn't give up now. He would be even more determined.

Chapter 19

Amelia was slow getting out of bed on Saturday morning. She felt lucky, though, to be only bruised and sore. Shivering to think of what might have been, she pulled on a robe and limped down to the kitchen.

"You made the headlines." Her father lingered over a second cup of coffee. "Thank God, you weren't hurt, Amelia. That stretch of road should be outlawed."

"Between the fog and the deer, it has to be the worst road in the state." Her mother agreed, hugging Amelia and handing her a cup of tea. "Are you sure you're all right? It's not too late to go in to the hospital and have a checkup."

"I'm sure, Mom. I'm just sore. We were lucky." If her parents knew the real cause of Garth's overturning his car, they'd take her to the police rather than the hospital.

She could hear the police laughing when Garth said, "A giant phantom football player emerged from the fog and spooked us." There were a lot of witnesses to the other two appearances of the ghost. So while they might laugh, someone might also investigate.

"Travis Westerman thinks the team's luck is running out." Mr. Seibert handed the newspaper to Amelia.

The headlines shouted the message of doom and gloom.

STONY BAY BOMBERS JINXED.
SHOULD TEAM CONTINUE SEASON?

A series of accidents has plagued the Bombers this season. Should Coach Paladino be more concerned about the safety of his players and less worried about his wins and losses?

The next couple of paragraphs detailed Buddy's getting burned, the signs all around Coach's house, the grill blowing up, Frank Evans's poisoning, and last, hers and Garth's accident.

Is this string of bad luck a coincidence? This reporter thinks otherwise. Along with the accidents, someone has continued a prank which started at the first pep rally for this year's team. A person dressed in Reggie Westerman's uniform has twice put in an appearance for members of the team. As many of you remember, Reggie was killed in an unfortunate accident at the final football game last year.

Is it possible that the jinx now plaguing the team started with Reggie? Should the team call off this year's season, even though they have a 4–0 record to date? Is there any connection between the appearance of the phantom player and these accidents?

It would seem strategic at this point for some investigation to take place, whether in an official form, or by the coach and members of his staff.

Of course there was some connection between members of the team getting hurt and appearances of the ghost. Amelia stood up.

"Where are you going, Amelia?" Mrs. Seibert stood at the table with a slice of hot toast in her hand. "Aren't you going to eat breakfast?"

"No time, Mom." Amelia grabbed the bread, smeared her mother's homemade raspberry jam on it generously, then bit into it as she hurried back to her room to get dressed.

She was going to find Garth immediately.

The phone rang just as she'd tugged on jeans and a sweatshirt. She grabbed it, hoping it was Garth. "Hello."

"Mel, it's me." Jilly's voice sounded more animated than it had in a long time. "Want to fly to Chicago today? Dad said we could ride along if we were ready within the hour. We can do some early Christmas shopping and get some new clothes."

Amelia was torn. It would be fun to go with Jilly. It might take her mind off what had been happening. And she and Jilly hadn't had much fun lately. But she lied.

"Jilly, I'm really tired and sore today. My ankle is hurting and I've got bruises on top of bruises. I'd love to, but maybe I'd better not."

"We could stop and eat every time you got tired."

"Then I'd outgrow the clothes before I even bought them."

"We could get cabs from store to store. I'll

pay. Daddy gave me extra allowance this week. And Mom got me a credit card of my very own. Isn't that incredible? I made a nuisance of myself until she gave in."

Amelia lied again. "Well, Mom keeps wanting me to get a checkup, so I may have to give in to her, and then I promised Garth I'd go over to the boat yard sometime today."

"I can't believe you're going to choose Garth over me again, Mel. You were with him last night." Her voice pouted.

"I'm not *choosing*, Jilly. Today just isn't a good day for me to go shopping."

"Okay. I may not invite you again." Jilly sounded as if she was only partly teasing.

"Let's plan a day ahead of time," Amelia said. "Okay?"

Jilly sighed. "I guess so, Mel. Bye."

Amelia tried not to feel guilty as she hurried downstairs again. "Can I take a car? I need to talk to Garth."

"Business at the store is picking up. Christmas shoppers, I guess. If your dad can take me to work, maybe Mrs. Hoff can drop me off when we close."

"Here, Mel." Her dad tossed his keys to her. "I'm going to stay right here all day and watch football."

Amelia caught the keys and threw him a kiss. "Thanks, Dad. Better come watch the Bombers next week. We have a home game."

"You don't think Pal is going to cancel the season?" He grinned.

"No way. He probably bribed Travis to write that article to lure the crowds in. Everyone in town will be there to see what happens next."

Cancelling the season was a great idea, Amelia thought as she drove over to the lake. She wished Coach would be sensible, but in her heart she knew it was the last thing he'd do.

"Did you read today's paper?" Mel asked Garth. "Travis thinks there's a connection between seeing the phantom player and the accidents." Amelia reminded Garth of all that had happened and the warnings they'd gotten beforehand.

"No one got hurt after the first pep rally. I don't know why, Mel, but I just think someone is trying to scare us or cause trouble. I wouldn't put it past Dougherty and the Lakers to be behind most of this. We've got them really worried now that we're winning without Reggie."

"Maybe once, Garth. But that seems like a lot of trouble to go to. Besides, Ralph Dougherty wasn't Reggie's ghost last night. They had their own game someplace."

"You're right, they did. Maybe they have someone who isn't on the team helping them."

"I think Travis Westerman can't stand to see anyone taking Reggie's place, playing as well at quarterback. He got rid of Buddy, and now he's after you."

"He may be angry, even protective of Reggie's reputation, but I can't believe he's the type of person that would deliberately hurt someone. I've known Travis as long as I've known Reggie. Reggie got all the attention at his house, but Travis seemed really proud of him."

"Sometimes grief makes people do strange things." Amelia stared out over the lake.

Garth was quiet for a long time. He seemed to be thinking about something. "Okay, Mel, I wasn't going to tell you, but look at this." Garth reached into the pocket of his shirt with two fingers, pulling out a folded scrap of paper. "This was stuck on the door this morning, in an envelope, with my name on it. I don't think Dad would have opened it, but I'm glad I found it first."

Amelia unfolded the half sheet of paper.

GARTH, YOU ARE A KILLER WHO HAS NEVER BEEN PUNISHED. YOU THINK

YOU GOT BY WITH KILLING REGGIE, DON'T YOU? AND NOW YOU ARE ALL PUFFED UP BECAUSE YOU HAVE TAKEN HIS PLACE. LUCK HAS SAVED YOU AGAIN AND AGAIN. REGGIE WAS NEVER THAT LUCKY. WE NEED TO TALK. MEET ME TONIGHT — IF YOU HAVE THE NERVE. I'LL BE WAITING FOR YOU ON REGGIE'S BOAT.

T.W.

"What are you going to do, Garth?"

"Nothing."

"Nothing? I can't believe you're going to ignore this." Amelia studied the block letters of the note as if they could tell her what to do. "Maybe you should give this note to the police. Let them take care of it. Tell them the truth about last night at the same time. Have you reported the accident?"

"Coach is going to take me back over there this afternoon." Garth put the note into his pocket. He picked up a wrench and stuck his nose back into the boat motor he was tinkering with.

"You're not going to show them the note, are you?"

"I think they'll laugh at me. And we don't

know for sure who sent this note. Anyone could have signed his initials. Look, Mel, I have to have my mind fully on the game this week. We nearly messed up last night. It would be embarrassing to lose now that we've come this far. And Coach would never forgive us. We'd never forgive ourselves."

"Pal is obsessed by winning and so are you, Garth."

"Cool it, Mel. I can take care of myself."

"Good!" Amelia got to her feet. "That means I can go shopping with Jilly." She glanced at her watch. "I can still catch her if I hurry."

She used the phone in the bait shop.

"Wow, you just caught me, Mel. We were going out the door."

"Will your dad wait fifteen minutes? And can I wear something of yours? I don't have time to go home and change."

"Sure." Jilly laughed. "You had a fight with Garth, didn't you? You did. I know you too well." When Amelia didn't answer, Jilly continued. "I'll call your mom and tell her where you'll be while you drive like mad to get here. Dad will wait if I beg."

She'd have to take Jilly's teasing, but it would be worth it. Amelia felt if she didn't get out of Stony Bay long enough to think, or stop thinking, she'd burst like a homecoming balloon.

But one decision came easy. She didn't think Garth was going to take that note seriously enough to call and tell Travis he wasn't keeping their appointment tonight. So Travis would meet Garth on Reggie's boat. He was going to be surprised when Amelia showed up instead.

Chapter 20

Jilly seemed unusually happy, and Amelia was glad she'd gone to Chicago with her. It was like old times. They shopped and ate and ate and shopped. And *most* of the day she managed to forget the reckless decision she'd made earlier in the morning.

When they were back at Jilly's, and Amelia stood at her car, Jilly hugged her extra tight.

"Oh, Mel." Jilly stepped away and stared at her. "I'm so glad you came with me. We've been drifting apart. But I want to remind you that you're the very best friend I've ever had."

"Hey," Amelia said, "you're acting like we'll never do this again."

"I — I still might go live with my aunt. In New York. Mom and I have been talking about it." Jilly's mind seemed to drift.

Amelia took her hand to pull her back. "But

this is our senior year, Jilly. You can't leave in the middle of senior year."

Jilly's face was pale. She had dark circles under her eyes. Was she sick? Amelia wondered. And keeping it secret?

"I might have to," Jilly said, finally.

"But why?"

"I — I'm just not happy. I've tried to be, but I'm not making much progress."

"You think moving to New York is going to make you happy?" Amelia asked.

"It might. At least I'd be away from — from what's happening."

"What happened last year is going to be inside you forever, Jilly." Amelia squeezed Jilly's hand. "You can't run away."

"I know that. I haven't run away from it."

"Then stay and tough out this year. It won't do you one bit of good to leave."

"It might." Jilly took a deep breath. "We'll talk more later. Bye."

Amelia got into her car, shrugged, then started the engine. She had something else to think about besides Jilly. Something foolish perhaps?

Her stomach started to churn when she sat down to dinner. It got worse by the minute.

Saying she was going to face up to Travis was one thing, doing it another.

You are a killer who has never been punished.

"You okay, Mel?" Mrs. Seibert asked. "It seems as if I'm always asking you that lately. But you're so quiet."

"I'm exhausted, Mom. Jilly probably put the limit on a new credit card in one day."

Mr. Seibert sipped his coffee. "Was Garth okay when you went over there this morning?"

"Yes, but I'm going back tonight. To pick him up," Amelia lied. She was certainly telling her quota of little lies lately. "Remember he doesn't have a car now."

"We may have to buy you a car yet." Amelia's dad heaped his plate with stew. It made Amelia's stomach lurch to watch. He handed her his car keys. "Be careful."

The docks were dark and quiet. Little hushes of water lapped the lakeshore and rocked boats. It was a sleepy, restful sound. Completely opposite from the way Amelia felt. Her heart pounded. Each step was carefully placed to make no noise.

Darkness magnified every sound. A rhythmical creaking of the rope holding Reggie's boat captive accompanied her stealthy progress. Finally she was ready to step from the dock onto the deck. She saw nothing but Reggie's rig. It wasn't a small sloop like the ones Garth and Jilly owned. It was larger, proudly displaying his name in gold letters across the bow.

She had dressed in a jean jacket like Garth's and had pulled on a watch cap so that, at a distance and at night, someone might mistake her for Garth. Glancing at the luminous dial on her watch, she saw she was exactly on time. *Okay, Travis. Where are you?*

Everything happened at once. A pop and a crisp sound fizzed behind her. *Whoomp!* Flames shot up around her, trapping her in the center of an inferno. Both hands flew up to protect her face. After a couple of seconds, she was too startled to scream, to make any sound other than the sharp intake of her breath.

Her eyes stung and her lungs felt raw and scorched. Suddenly, a dark figure was backlighted by the red, yellow, and blue flames. She stood, riveted to the boat dock. Her heart hammered wildly, throbbed in her temples until she felt dizzy. Frantically, she looked for a way to escape, both from the person coming toward her and the fire.

Before she could move, the figure flew

through the air toward her, perfectly aimed, like a Bay Bombers' tackle.

"Oooof." She grunted with the painful impact of his body with hers. Then she sailed out over the water, empty space all around her. She hit the water with a *smack*. It was cold, and solid as a sheet of glass. Until she began to sink. Waves slapped her face.

Icy liquid closed over her head.

Chapter 21

When she gained consciousness, she found herself still in the water, being held by arms stronger than she would have guessed belonged to a reporter. Travis was trying to drown her!

"Let me go, Travis, let me go!" She struggled to break his hold, pounding on his chest with both fists.

Breaking loose, she fought the water, kicked in a frantic version of swimming until she got her feet under her near the shore. She waded, but the water seemed to grip her legs, resisting her every step. She stumbled, fell, forgetting to close her mouth. The water tasted fishy and oily, stale and muddy. She spit and coughed. Her stomach roiled, wanting to turn inside out.

The splashing behind her said Travis followed. "Mel, wait! Talk to me."

She had come to talk, to reason with him. What a joke. *Please don't try to kill me, Travis — or to kill Garth*, she would have said. Hollow words. *The explosion was meant for Garth.*

He grabbed her arm as she swung it backward for a balance. She twisted it painfully, trying to wrench free. "Let me go, Travis, let go!"

"Okay, okay. Some thanks I get for saving your life." Travis released her. She swung around, stumbling onto the shore. Flames behind her roared toward the sky. Heat waves parched her face and lips.

Travis followed her out of the water. She kept some distance between them.

"What do you mean, saving my life? You nearly drowned me. First you set a trap for Garth, then I suppose you realized I wasn't Garth. You didn't mean to kill *me*."

She had a terrible impulse to laugh, but she tightened her fists to keep control. She shivered, despite the heat, the inferno so close to shore.

"What are you talking about, Amelia? I don't want to kill anyone."

"You expect me to believe that?"

"I don't expect anything except an explanation. What were you doing on Reggie's boat? At this time of night? Why are you babbling about my trying to kill Garth? Were you meeting someone here?" He fired off questions like the ambitious reporter getting a story.

"What were *you* doing on Reggie's boat?" she asked.

"Pardon me, but it's my boat now. I have a right to be there. I come down here a lot at night."

"You — you didn't set it afire?"

"Why would I do a fool thing like that?"

"What happened, Travis? Tell me what happened out there tonight. Everything you saw or heard." Amelia kept her distance from Travis, watched him carefully, but she needed to get him to talk to her.

"Now who's asking the questions?"

"This is important, Travis. Just answer them."

"I stayed late at the paper, got the Sunday edition on the presses, then found I wasn't the least bit tired — not the kind of tired it takes to sleep. I was going to sit here on the water for awhile." He paused.

His explanation seemed truthful, but she stepped away from him again. In the distance, sirens wailed. Help was coming.

"So you came onto the boat. Did you see anyone?"

No. I was about to speak to you, to ask you what you were doing on Reggie's boat. Suddenly, flames raced across the deck and collided with that can of gasoline. I thought I smelled gas when I stepped on the deck, but I didn't see anything then, except you. I thought you were trying to steal the boat."

"Steal your boat?"

He stepped toward her. She stepped back.

"There was a story in the Waukegan paper about a ring of thieves ripping off small boats the last couple of weeks."

"Did you know who I was?"

"Not from the back. When you turned around, I recognized you. At the same time I knew we both had to get out of there." Travis stepped toward her again. She stepped back two steps.

If Travis didn't set the fire, who did? She glanced behind her. Shadows, only shadows. Anyone could be out there, watching them. Waiting for another chance.

Footsteps pounded toward them.

"Amelia, there you are. What happened?" Suddenly Garth stood beside them. "The boat — the fire — are you hurt?" He took

Amelia's arm and spun her around. She tried to tug away from Garth, too. He held her captive.

"I'm okay, Garth. Travis got me off the boat when it caught fire." She'd give Travis credit for that. Maybe he set the trap, but when he saw the wrong person in it, he got her out.

"Oh, Mel, why did you come down here by yourself?" Garth scolded her. "That was foolish."

"I came because you wouldn't, Garth. Someone has to find out what's going on." She didn't like being called foolish. "Someone had to find out who wrote that note."

"What note?" asked Travis.

Garth looked at Amelia, who shrugged. "Someone sent me a note to meet him here tonight, Travis. He signed your initials."

"You got a note to meet *me* here? Let me see it."

"I tore it up," Garth said. "I chose to ignore it."

"Then what are you doing here?" Amelia asked. Her teeth chattered and she was shaking. Could Garth have set the fire?

"I called and your mother said you'd gone to meet me. It took me only a few minutes to figure out where you'd really gone."

"You were a little late, Dreyer," Travis said. "If I hadn't been here, your girlfriend would be dead. Maybe the real Stony Bay jinx is being associated with you."

Garth's hand tightened on her arm. "Or believing the stories you make up to cover for yourself. I don't know what your motive is for wanting to kill me, Travis, but since the police are here now, we'll let them decide who's responsible for this."

"Suits me fine, Dreyer. I'm reporting arson, person unknown. Trespassing on Amelia's part, and destroying evidence on your part. You'd better get your story ready." Travis started toward his car. "But to remind you that I'm a compassionate person, Amelia, I have a blanket in my trunk to keep you from freezing while we get to the bottom of this."

Amelia was so mixed up, she didn't know what to believe. It had occurred to her that the only other person on the dock tonight was Garth. He had guessed that she'd be here. He had showed up within minutes of the explosion. He could easily have been here all along.

She'd take the blanket. She'd tell the police what happened tonight. But she felt she might never be warm again.

Chapter 22

On Monday, despite her fear and confusion about Saturday night — the police had decided nothing — Amelia sat on the low wall outside the tunnel to the locker room. She waited for Garth to come out. Where was he? It was almost dark.

She suffered through the embarrassment of suggestive remarks by the other players.

"Go help him, Mel."

"Yeah, he'd like his back scrubbed."

"He's depressed. Coach was on his case about being slow today. Go raise his pulse a few notches."

Soon it seemed that everyone had gone, but still Garth lingered. The late afternoon was losing its light quickly. The day grew chilly, a cold breeze coming from the west. She shivered with her own cold thoughts.

She was going over and over her list of suspects. Captain Warsaw, from the police department, asked her to meet with him again and go over every event of the past weeks. She had come up with five people who had motive and opportunity to hurt the Bomber players, if she included Ralph Dougherty from the Lakers.

Travis was still at the top of the list despite his saying he saved her life on Saturday night. He was a really smooth talker.

Travis had kept her suspicions about Garth alive. Right now she sat waiting for Garth. Could she really trust him? It got even darker and colder. She glanced at her watch. She'd give him five more minutes. She hadn't seen Coach come out either. She didn't want to interrupt their talking, especially if he was angry and chewing Garth out.

She knew Garth wasn't the phantom football player. She had seen him on the stage when the Phantom appeared the first time. She had been with him the other two times.

Shelby was her number one suspect for being the Phantom. He had the theatrical know-how to create the appearances. And he hated football players, jocks. Hated them even more after the incident at Coach's party where they'd humiliated him, stuffing him in the trash barrel. But how far could hate go? A long way once it got started, she knew.

Or Coach Pal. How far would he go to win? A long way, she suspected, yet, surely he wouldn't be hurting his own players. Would he?

Amelia glanced at her watch again. Where *was* Garth? Something had happened to him! The idea pulled her to her feet. She wasn't waiting for him any longer. She pushed through the locker-room door and looked around. Damp air from the showers hung heavy in the room along with the smell of sweaty bodies, leather, shaving lotion. She walked slowly and quietly around a row of lockers.

Garth was dressed but sat slumped on a bench.

"What's wrong, Garth?" Amelia could tell by his face that something had happened again.

"Mel, what are you doing here? Get out. Now."

"I will not. I've been waiting for you ever since practice ended. We're going to the police station. Remember?"

"Go on home. I'll call you. We'll go later."

"Garth, I'm not leaving. I'm not walking one step away from you until you tell me what's wrong."

Garth sighed and opened his hand. "I found this note in my locker when I went to practice. I've been thinking about it ever since. Coach hassled me for two hours because my mind wasn't on the field." Garth handed Amelia the wadded paper.

She smoothed it out and read.

ESCAPED AGAIN, DIDN'T YOU? YOU SENT MEL TO MEET ME. THAT WAS NEARLY A FATAL MISTAKE — ANOTHER FATAL MISTAKE. SURELY YOU COULDN'T HAVE LIVED WITH THAT, TOO. HOW MANY PEOPLE ARE YOU GOING TO TAKE DOWN WITH YOU, GARTH? STAY AND FACE UP TO ME, IF YOU HAVE THE GUTS. I'LL COME TO THE LOCKER ROOM AFTER EVERYONE ELSE IS GONE.

Amelia glanced around quickly. The hot, damp air became heavy, oppressive. A shiver raced the length of her spine and raised the tiny hairs on the back of her neck.

"Mel, this is my problem. I want you out of here." Garth stood, pulled her up against him, and whispered.

She whispered back. "It's mine, too, Garth. I'm not leaving."

Neither of them moved when they heard the sound of cleats on the tiled floor. She never considered going toward the sound. Let it come to them.

Garth's fingers cut into her shoulders as he tightened his hold on her. She leaned into him. She imagined she felt his heart pounding through his chest and against her back.

He pushed her around behind him, holding her there with one arm. She struggled to get loose. She wasn't hiding behind him. At least that was her thought until the lights went out. Her body tensed. She gripped Garth's arm.

The locker room plunged into darkness as thick as the humid air, darkness you could reach out and touch. She wanted to pull it aside like you'd pull back a curtain so you could see out.

They stood together, frozen, until the clicking footsteps came around the row of lockers.

It was almost a relief when the spotlight the Phantom Player carried flooded Reggie Westerman with bright yellow rays. The number nine glowed gold against the black jersey. The figure didn't seem quite as tall as it had on stage or coming up out of the lake, but it was just as awesome, just as imposing.

Most frightening, though, was the object in

the ghost player's left hand. And the fact that Amelia had seen it before.

She didn't know much about guns. Ordinarily she wouldn't recognize one over another. But she remembered thinking that it was a shame that something so beautifully crafted could be so deadly.

The tiny, thirty-two caliber handgun called a Seecamp, an exclusive make, expensive, special ordered and hard to get, pointed straight at Garth's heart.

Chapter 23

Amelia gripped Garth's shoulder and spoke. "Shelby, you don't want to shoot Garth. Put the gun down."

"Shelby?" Garth whispered.

The figure hesitated. The gloved hand that held the gun wavered slightly. The scene froze, balanced in time, in place.

Amelia gained confidence, lost some of her fear, as Shelby did nothing. She stepped in front of Garth. It was a gamble, but she didn't think Shelby would shoot her. And he might shoot Garth. That was what he came for. He'd prepared for violence by stealing the gun.

"Amelia, don't!" Garth shoved her aside.

Immediately the light snapped off, the gun and the spotlight clattered to the floor. Cleats clicked across the tile as the ghost ran for the opposite locker-room door, the one that led to the gymnasium.

"Quick, Garth. Follow him. We have to stop him."

Instead of wasting time asking questions, Garth dashed for the door to the gym. He flipped on the locker-room lights as he went through, then slowed as they entered the huge, dark, empty cavern of a room.

"Where are the lights?" Amelia whispered. "Do you know?" Her whisper echoed, *know, know, know*.

The ghost had stopped running. To the left there was a muffled shuffling, puzzling and impossible to identify.

"I think so. Stay here." Garth left her.

The minute she was alone, Amelia started to shake. She was cold, freezing. She might as well be standing outside in the dead of a Michigan winter. The tiny sounds echoed across the gym and back again. The scraping — now it was overhead. Something dropped, bounced near her with a thump. She jumped back, looking up as if her eyes would get used to the dense blackness.

All around her the smell of freshly waxed wood filled her nostrils. In the silent air hung recent echoes of screams, shouts, feet thumping, whistles blowing, the laughter of games played, won, lost. Where was Garth? Why was he taking so long?

When the lights flooded the gymnasium, she was looking at one black shoe with cleats. Quickly, she raised her head and stared. The figure of Reggie was sprawled on one of the steel girders, inching its way along. One of the fat knotted ropes hung close to it. Shelby had climbed the rope. But there was no way to escape from overhead.

"Shelby, come down," Amelia called. Her voice echoed about the room. "Come back down the rope. Garth has called the police. You can't get away, so just come down. I'll wait with you. We'll talk."

Garth hadn't called the police, but Shelby wouldn't know that. Out of the corner of her eye, Amelia saw that Garth had climbed a ladder on the wall near the bank of lights. There was a catwalk around the ceiling. Following it to the beam where the player balanced, lying flat, he bent and eased himself onto the girder.

Is that the right thing to do, Garth? Amelia couldn't think straight. Could Garth grab Shelby before he fell — or jumped?

And why should Garth risk his life for Shelby? He had tried to kill Garth, more than once. They could struggle and both fall.

The shuffling sounds Garth made, sliding along, carried across the hollow dome. Shelby stopped, glanced back.

"Stop where you are, Garth. Don't come any closer to me."

That voice! Verging on hysteria. *It wasn't Shelby's!*

Garth froze. Amelia's hands squeezed into fists at her sides. Her stomach tightened. She had never felt so sick, so helpless.

The Phantom Player kicked off the other shoe, wrapped both legs around the beam, inching forward again. Pulling off the helmet, the Phantom dropped it, watching it bounce.

Amelia screamed. "Jilly! No, no, no! It can't be. Please, oh, no, Jilly, no!"

All the tenseness, all the fear, and now the horror caught up with Amelia. She started to cry uncontrollably, staring at Jilly sprawled on the steel girder. Over and over she mumbled, "No, no, no, no!" Not Jilly. Not Jilly!

She had to stop crying. She had to do something. Shaking, gasping for air, she struggled to gain control. "Jilly." Her voice shook. "Jilly." It was stronger. "Keep going, Jilly. Come down the other side. We'll talk. We can work this out."

"We can't either. Reggie wants you both punished."

"Why, Jilly, why? And how do you know what Reggie wants? Reggie is gone, Jilly, gone." Amelia wasn't sure what to say, but she wanted to keep Jilly talking.

"He's not gone! He's here. You just can't see him. But *I* can. That's why he asked me to help him, to be him. He's with me now, helping me punish you. You have to be punished because you're happy, and he's not. He's so unhappy, Mel. If you could only feel his pain."

Jilly sat up, her long white hair tumbling around her face wildly. Her eyes, wide and glazed, stared, trancelike, across the gym. Was she forgetting where she was?

"Jilly, listen to me. Let Reggie go. He wants to go on now. That's the only way he can be happy. He's ready. You have to stop being Reggie and start being you again." Amelia stretched her hand, reached for Jilly even though she was high overhead.

"Reggie doesn't want to go. He wants to come back."

"He can't come back." Amelia glanced to the left. Garth was edging closer, closer.

"Then I have to go with him, Mel. We can't be separated now."

Amelia was never sure how it happened. Just that it did. Maybe Jilly let go intentionally. In slow motion she slipped, rolled off the beam. She grabbed at it with both hands, but she was still wearing the gloves that had hidden her long slender fingers while she played "Reggie."

She clung for a couple of seconds. Garth crawled toward her, but it was impossible to hurry across the narrow beam. Letting go, Jilly fell. Down, down, down. It must have taken only seconds for her to hit the wooden floor with the huge thump of her body and the crash of shoulder pads, but her fall seemed to last forever.

Chapter 24

Amelia ran, knelt beside Jilly. Long blonde hair flowed around Jilly's face. Her eyes were closed, long lashes curled, wet. In the glare of the harsh gym lights, her face was milky marble softened only by a soft slash of pink on her lips.

"Jilly, Jilly, please, please open your eyes." Carefully Amelia put both hands alongside Jilly's face, not wanting to move her, but wanting Jilly to know she was there.

Jilly moaned. She wasn't dead! Her eyes flew open. She stared at Amelia as if wondering what happened.

"Oh, Jilly. Why did you do this?"

"I can't move, Mel. Why can't I move?"

"Don't try, Jilly. We're getting help."

"Reggie, where is Reggie? He'll help me." Jilly squeezed her eyes tight. "He's gone, Mel! Reggie, where are you?"

Amelia wept, softly now, letting tears roll down her cheeks, spotting the black jersey with the big number nine. She stared at Jilly whose eyes glazed as if she were a long way off.

"Reggie is dead, Jilly. Remember? Last year?"

"I wanted to hurt everyone who hurt him." Jilly came back. "People . . . tried to take his place, to be better than he was. I couldn't let that happen. I couldn't let his fans forget him."

Amelia tugged off one brown glove and squeezed Jilly's hand, not knowing if she could feel anything. Her palms were moist, but freezing cold.

"No one hurt Reggie on purpose," Amelia reminded Jilly. "It was an accident, Jilly, an accident."

"No, Garth could have stopped it. Garth should have protected Reggie."

"You helped Reggie as much as you could, Jilly. Now you have to help yourself. You have to stop thinking about Reggie."

"How can I? I don't want to live anymore without . . . without Reggie."

Amelia glanced around, but didn't see Garth. He must have gone for help. Who she *did* see, to her surprise, was Shelby.

He ran to them. "Jilly, no, oh no, Jilly. What happened, Amelia? I was following her, but she lost me."

"She fell from the girder, Shelby," Amelia explained. "She's hurt badly."

Shelby knelt beside Jilly, took her other hand. "Jilly, hang on. Please be all right. I love you, Jilly."

Jilly laughed. "I know you do, Gumby, but I could never love anyone but Reggie. I needed your help, but you can't love me." Jilly closed her eyes.

"You helped her be the Phantom, didn't you, Shelby?" Amelia asked, needing to know the whole story now that she knew the terrible truth.

"She asked me to help her stage Reggie's appearance at the pep rally. It was supposed to be a *joke*. A joke. I thought it was a great idea." Shelby stared at Jilly, squeezing her hand.

"Where did she get a football uniform?"

"In Chicago. She had a costume place make one like Reggie's. It was easy to stage. She came in the backdoor after getting the stuff out of her car."

"Coach spoiled it," Jilly said. She wasn't unconscious. "He used my idea. Just like he used

Reggie. He pushed Reggie all the time." She coughed and choked.

"Don't try to talk, Jilly." Amelia said.

"I — I need to tell you this, Mel." She paused, swallowed. "Reggie said Coach Pal would kill him if the Bombers didn't win. He did . . . Coach Pal killed Reggie. He made him play when he was sick."

"She hates Paladino," Shelby added. "She made me help her put those signs all over his property at the party. I was worried about her, so I did. It seemed harmless."

"You think she poured gas on Garth's grill?" Amelia asked.

"Yes." Shelby stared at Jilly. "I'm glad he wasn't hurt."

"How did you get Reggie to come up out of the water?" asked Amelia, looking around. Where was Garth, the ambulance?

"We used her and her father's scuba gear. I had a spotlight, but the moon was so bright, I didn't use it. Then when she rose out of the water, I stayed under, out deeper, waiting to take the costume and put it back into the sailboat. Jilly's an incredible swimmer." Shelby patted Jilly's hand.

"She swam down the shoreline and came out where no one saw her," Amelia guessed. "We were all looking for Reggie. When you came out of the water, Shelby, I thought you'd been looking for Reggie, too. You'd been in the water all the time."

"It was easy." Shelby said. "Everyone was so freaked out. No one was paying attention to me."

"Did you push Buddy into the fire, Jilly?" Amelia figured she'd better hear that, too, no matter how awful it was. Jilly. She still couldn't believe it. She didn't want to believe it.

"I didn't mean to . . . to hurt him so badly. Just to keep him from stealing Reggie's place. He was too good. So was Garth. I had to stop Garth, too. Everyone would have forgotten Reggie."

Amelia had the rest of the story. "And you poisoned Garth's shoulder pads, not knowing Frank would wear them instead?"

"I didn't know she was doing those things, Amelia." Shelby frowned. "I didn't know she hurt Buddy. No one was supposed to get hurt. When I started to suspect, when I accused her of actually hurting someone, she denied it."

"But you knew, didn't you?" Amelia felt sorry for Shelby. Jilly was good at getting people to do what she wanted. She had always been spoiled.

"I realized — I realized, she didn't always *know* what she was doing, that she was sick." Very carefully, Shelby had said that Jilly was losing her mind. Amelia knew that. The Jilly who had been her friend would never deliberately hurt someone.

Jilly laughed, choked. "You would do anything for me, wouldn't you, Gumby? You hate jocks. But you fell in love with me. That wasn't in the plan. You're so gullible, Gumby. Did you really think I could love you back? Reggie will always be my true love. I'm going to die, aren't I, Mel? Then I'll be with Reggie forever." Jilly's words ran together and her voice got weaker.

"You stepped in front of Garth on the highway, didn't you, Jilly?" Amelia ignored what Jilly had said about dying. She *had* to know the whole story.

"Yes. I thought of that. I didn't need Shelby anymore, but I couldn't get him to go away, to leave me alone. Turns out I did need him to go back to White Cloud to get my car."

"You told me you had a flat, Jilly. Reggie appeared again?" Shelby asked Amelia.

"Garth kept being lucky. I'm going to die without punishing him and he killed Reggie," Jilly said.

"You're not going to die, Jilly. You have to live. You have to take responsibility for all you've done." Amelia wasn't sure Jilly was going to live, but she didn't want Jilly to give up.

"I nearly killed you, Mel. I'm sorry." Jilly stopped talking, trying to get her breath. Tears rolled down her cheeks.

Amelia brushed away the tears. "Hush, Jilly. You don't have to say any more."

"I — I do. Why did you come to Reggie's boat, Mel? I thought you were Garth. I had to wait there in the water, seeing Travis pull you out. Garth got away from me again. You've stopped being my friend, Mel. All you care about is Garth. You just want to be with Garth. You know I don't have anyone."

"Hush, Jilly," Amelia said, looking at Shelby. Tears ran down his face. He made no move to wipe them away. Why wasn't someone coming to help them?

Finally Garth hurried through the locker-room door. He knelt beside them. "I called an ambulance. It's coming. Will she be all right?"

Jilly had closed her eyes again. She appeared to be struggling to breathe.

"I don't know, Garth. I don't know. But if

she does, she may be paralyzed — like Reggie would have been."

"Jilly!" Shelby squeezed her hand. "We're losing her, Amelia."

"When did Shelby come in?" Garth whispered.

Shelby heard him. "I followed her. I saw her leave home in that costume. I knew I had to stop her, but she drove so fast, and my car — my stupid car — " He smoothed Jilly's hair back away from her face. "She's so beautiful. And such a good actress. We both had you fooled, didn't we?"

"Yes, Shelby. I suspected you, but never Jilly. I wish you'd have told me what was happening," Amelia said.

"She said she'd never see me again if I told anyone. And I didn't know *everything*. I didn't know how — how — desperate for revenge she'd become. She pretended she loved me."

"She was crazy about Reggie." Amelia wished she hadn't used that word. Anger, bitterness, grief had stolen the Jilly she had known. In her place was this person who was desperate and without a conscience.

Amelia leaned into Garth, but didn't cry anymore. She watched as the EMTs arrived and lifted Jilly to a stretcher and placed her on a metal cart. Amelia turned to Garth. "Oh, Garth, can you forgive me?"

"For what, Mel?"

"I suspected you of hurting Buddy and Frank. Travis put that into my mind. And I was so confused and scared."

"I know, Mel, I know." Garth held her tight. "I was so scared, I almost let you get killed. I ignored that note to come to Reggie's boat, not knowing you'd go. You're the one who needs to forgive me."

They followed the EMTs outside. Shelby walked beside the cart where Jilly lay. As they paused behind the ambulance, one of the men reached over and touched Jilly.

Amelia broke away from Garth and ran to Jilly. "Can I go with her?" she asked. "She's my best friend."

The young man's eyes were sad. "I'm sorry, Miss. She won't need you now." He pulled the sheet up over Jilly's face.

Amelia stepped back as if someone had hit her. Biting her lip, she pressed her hand to her mouth to keep from screaming out. Jilly didn't need anyone now. Not her. Not Shelby, who stood alone, staring at the men as they lifted the stretcher into the ambulance.

Amelia turned to Garth, and he held her close again. She would get through this night. Then she'd have to face each day ahead, missing Jilly and wishing she could have helped her.

THRILLERS

R.L. Stine
☐ MC44236-8 The Baby-sitter $3.50
☐ MC44332-1 The Baby-sitter II $3.50
☐ MC46099-4 The Baby-sitter III $3.50
☐ MC45386-6 Beach House $3.25
☐ MC43278-8 Beach Party $3.50
☐ MC43125-0 Blind Date $3.50
☐ MC43279-6 The Boyfriend $3.50
☐ MC44333-X The Girlfriend $3.50
☐ MC45385-8 Hit and Run $3.25
☐ MC46100-1 The Hitchhiker $3.50
☐ MC43280-X The Snowman $3.50
☐ MC43139-0 Twisted $3.50

Caroline B. Cooney
☐ MC44316-X The Cheerleader $3.25
☐ MC41641-3 The Fire $3.25
☐ MC43806-9 The Fog $3.25
☐ MC45681-4 Freeze Tag $3.25
☐ MC45402-1 The Perfume $3.25
☐ MC44884-6 The Return of the
Vampire $2.95
☐ MC41640-5 The Snow $3.25
☐ MC45682-2 The Vampire's
Promise $3.50

Diane Hoh
☐ MC44330-5 The Accident $3.25
☐ MC45401-3 The Fever $3.25
☐ MC43050-5 Funhouse $3.25
☐ MC44904-4 The Invitation $3.50
☐ MC45640-7 The Train $3.25

Sinclair Smith
☐ MC45063-8 The Waitress $2.95

Christopher Pike
☐ MC43014-9 Slumber Party $3.50
☐ MC44256-2 Weekend $3.50

A. Bates
☐ MC45829-9 The Dead
Game $3.25
☐ MC43291-5 Final Exam $3.25
☐ MC44582-0 Mother's Helper $3.50
☐ MC44238-4 Party Line $3.25

D.E. Athkins
☐ MC45246-0 Mirror, Mirror $3.25
☐ MC45349-1 The Ripper $3.25
☐ MC44941-9 Sister Dearest $2.95

Carol Ellis
☐ MC46411-6 Camp Fear $3.25
☐ MC44768-8 My Secret
Admirer $3.25
☐ MC46044-7 The Stepdaughter $3.25
☐ MC44916-8 The Window $2.95

Richie Tankersley Cusick
☐ MC43115-3 April Fools $3.25
☐ MC43203-6 The Lifeguard $3.25
☐ MC43114-5 Teacher's Pet $3.25
☐ MC44235-X Trick or Treat $3.25

Lael Littke
☐ MC44237-6 Prom Dress $3.25

Edited by T. Pines
☐ MC45256-8 Thirteen $3.50

Available wherever you buy books, or use this order form.

Scholastic Inc., P.O. Box 7502, 2931 East McCarty Street, Jefferson City, MO 65102

Please send me the books I have checked above. I am enclosing $_____ (please add
$2.00 to cover shipping and handling). Send check or money order — no cash or C.O.D.s please.

Name _____ Birthdate _____

Address_____

City_____ State/Zip_____
Please allow four to six weeks for delivery. Offer good in the U.S. only. Sorry, mail orders are not
available to residents of Canada. Prices subject to change.

T193